THE BOY WHO PLAYED THE QUEEN

ALSO AVAILABLE

THE SLOE MOON SERIES

Volume 1: Tall Trees
Volume 2: Stoneharp
Volume 3: Crooked Hill
Volume 4: Eastbay
Volume 5: Halfway (July 2025)
Volume 6: Goldenlake (November 2025)

COMING SOON

THE SUN & FLAME DUOLOGY (FROM 2026)

Volume 1: Everything the Sun Touches
Volume 2: Everything the Flame Heals

CONTENT WARNINGS

strong language, alcoholism, infidelity

THE BOY WHO PLAYED THE QUEEN

A SEAGARD NOVELLA

C. M. KUHTZ

WOLLSCHWEBER

PUBLISHING

Wollschweber Publishing
www.wollschweberpublishing.com

CREDITS
Copyediting: River Ari, Better Than Sex Editing
Production: C. M. Kuhtz
Cover design: C. M. Kuhtz
Cover image: Nick Hughes
Logo design: Dorit Osang
Interior illustrations: Ken Turner

A catalogue record for this book is available from the British Library.

ISBN 978-1-0683196-8-6 paperback
ISBN 978-1-0683196-9-3 ebook

AUTHOR NOTE

Some have read my books and are familiar with the world of the Eight Kingdoms, but I hope you find the introductory notes useful. *The Boy Who Played the Queen* is the first full-length English-language text based in the Eight Kingdoms that I ever wrote. It was my Nanowrimo project for 2020, when the UK was deep in lockdowns and my usual writing routines were totally disrupted. I had half-heartedly published four German-language trilogies in ebook format, always feeling guilty about spending so much time on these projects. I had lived in the UK for a few years at that point and knew that my German grammar was taking a hit. It was time to switch to English.

The Boy became a test to gauge how fast I could write in a language I lived with but that wasn't truly mine. It came with unexpected ease and quite quickly. Originally, I had planned for *The Boy* to be 15,000 words, a fragment of sorts, explaining the origin story of the actors Faral and Tjor, two supporting characters from an earlier novel. In the end, I wrote over 35,000 words and kept the story in the back of my mind, in case I wanted to do more with it.

At its heart, *The Boy* is a simple, romantic story set in a low fantasy universe. It plays out among people who would be background characters in other novels, people who don't encounter magic and whose problems very much resemble our own. On rereading *The Boy* in 2024, I decided to revisit the text. At that point, I had finished ten English-language manuscripts, had gone through beta-reading and copyediting processes for six of them, and found that I still liked this story a lot.

While everything I wrote later is set in an early medieval time, *The Boy* connects to the German projects set in an early modern period, which means the city of Seagard is a very different place than in the *Sloe Moon* series and subsequent books. There are lemons and chocolate, plus other foods that wouldn't have been available earlier, and while the legends and places stay more or less the same, the people in Seagard live very different lives. Its theatre scene is closely oriented to sixteenth-century English history, with the same stipulation that women are not allowed to play female characters. The city has grown and is firmly in the grip of four companies trading with the rest of the known world—maps have expanded, tastes diversified, and what were once eight separate kingdoms have merged into one realm, ruled from Pietwood Castle in what was Whiterivers territory in *Sloe Moon*.

One of the joys of writing multiple novels in the same storyverse is exploring various points of history and filling in the gaps. Things have changed, but I'm still figuring out how events have come to pass. While *Sloe Moon* and the upcoming *Sun & Flame* duology are set in a period when magic is returning to the world and flaring up in unexpected ways, Faral and Tjor live in much quieter times, when magic has ebbed away again. The plays that form an integral piece of this story hark back to the mythical age when magic was abundant; through them, magic features in *The Boy*. The stories referenced in the plays are also threads that weave throughout all my books, and if you've read one or two of them, you might recognize some of their motives. I hope you enjoy seeing these familiar landscapes in a new light.

PART I

FARAL &
THE HILLAKES

1
RUIN THE STORY

I T HAD RAINED FOR weeks in the Hillakes, and the path the two boys followed down the ridge to Halfway was slippery under their leather soles. Faral, who everyone always called Far, had already fallen twice and planned to wash his hands in the horse trough as soon as they reached the coach station.

"I'm sure they'll ruin it," he grumbled.

"You still want to pay and see it?" Cas asked.

"It's my favourite story ever—of course I'll pay and see it!"

Far held strong opinions about how the fairy tales he'd grown up with should be told, and he never hesitated to inform everyone about it. How could a troupe of players from gods-knows-where be trusted with legends so rooted in the Hillakes?

On their way down the slopes, the boys passed grazing sheep and the cream-coloured ponies the district was famous for. The clumps of dark, thorny gorse bushes that cluttered the landscape were slowly coming back into flower, and from time to time their sweet scent reached the boys.

Both Far and Cas had spent their entire lives, such as they were, in the Hillakes, and while Cas didn't seem to mind, Far very much wished to leave both the hills and the lakes behind. The village of Halfway, with its coach station, smithies, and repair shops, was the largest settlement in this part of the district. Even without the additional enticement of the players coming east for the spring festivals, Far had always thought the walk over the high ridge from Sheepdip-on-Lightwater well worth the effort, despite the risk of travelling a few lengths downhill on your bum.

His father would rather see him take an interest in the village he actually lived in, but by now he knew his youngest son well enough not to be too disappointed in his strange fascination with the travellers at the station, with the exhausted-looking gentlemen and veiled ladies who spent the night so desperately wishing they were someplace else. For them, Halfway was a muddy yard; a dark taproom that smelled of smoke, woodchips, and strong beer; and a few hours of uneasy sleep before the coach stood again at the ready.

For Far, Halfway meant half a day without the sheep, a whiff of spice mixed into meat pies, and a peek into all the lives he would never lead—not as the youngest boy of the shepherd at Riverbend Farm, the one who had to bribe his friend to see the players because not even Cas knew why he absolutely had to come and watch them.

One of Far's brothers had brought the flyer home last week, and Far had ripped it out of his hand:

THE QVEEN VNDER THE LAKE

He'd read the poorly printed scrap a few times, the tip of his finger touching every woodcut letter, his breath catching in his throat.

He could still remember the first time his grandmother had told him the story. It differed from the versions he heard later because his grandmother could do the voices of all the characters, including the Evil Duke, and Far had always suspected that something in the way she spoke the Queen's words was meant to paint her a little less mad.

He remembered asking himself the question, "What would I do if I was married to the Cruel King?" Whenever he found himself on the lakeshore, squeezed between the steep sides of the valley that formed the backdrop to the Lightwater lake, he wondered whether a life below the water could be so much worse than a life among the sheep.

Cas had always sided with the King, as was expected. Both boys were the youngest sons of their fathers, but Cas's family ran the mill in Sheepdip, and many of the villagers found it a bit odd that he had time for the boy who lived at Riverbend. His brothers had long since mocked him for putting up with Far's weird ramblings and his talk about queens, princes, and waterhorses.

They were the only boys of the same age in Sheepdip and felt deeply resentful towards their fathers. Far had had a crush on Cas ever since the sheep dipping last year, when Cas had tried to save him from being trampled by Riverbend's old ram and received a cloven hoof for his troubles, right in the fruits. Lately Cas had tried to ignore him a few times, and that stung worse than falling into a gorse bush, but an afternoon at the station was too good to pass up.

Far had promised to pay for the play and the beer. He'd kept the two copperlings back for a long time, because the players always came for the festival, and after seeing them for the first time five years ago, there was no way he could stay back in Sheepdip when the torches around the stage were lit just over the ridge.

They were lucky with the weather; the last snow had melted under the incessant rains of the first spring months, and from time to time a glimpse of blue sky showed in the Northwater below them. Halfway had been settled a long time ago, built on an island accessible by two broad stone bridges, one in the east, one in the west, cutting the surrounding lake into South- and Northwater. Most of the houses belonged to the station, but there was Halfway Manor, hidden behind oak trees on the highest point of the island, though visible from the ridge. Most of the time it seemed to be empty, because the master of Halfway was an inkling in Seagard, a man who wrote for his living, and therefore someone whom all the families in Sheepdip were deeply suspicious of.

Far and Cas were able to read the flyer from the station and scratch their names in the mud with a stick, but none of the boys in Sheepdip could write properly. Their stories were told at the fireside by women who were constantly spinning or preparing fleece. Even Cas's mother and sisters had to spin, and none of them had ever put quill to paper.

Far and Cas hiked down the slope to the Eastbridge, scraped the mud off their shoes on the milestone that marked the halfway point from Seagard to Pietwood Castle, and ran the last bit to the ring of outbuildings forming the station yard, where torches had been placed in a square and sand thrown down to dry the stage for the players. The barn served as the back area where the players changed into their wigs and costumes. More flyers were glued to the gateposts, featuring the same letters, the same print of the Queen under the waves of the Lightwater.

A lot of people were already waiting, clay tankards in hand, and they all talked about the story. "The Queen under the Lake" was a well-known tale, and Far wasn't the only one excited by the prospect of seeing it performed just a stone's throw from the actual lake where it supposedly happened.

Cas was clearly nervous, wrestling with his voice to keep it from squeaking. "Where do we buy the beer?"

Far made his way to the horse trough, rubbed his hands clean, and dried his fingers by raking them through his long brown hair. "We'll probably have to go inside."

"Are you sure we should? Looks like the taproom is crammed."

Far shrugged. "Stay here if you want to."

He couldn't remember ever having seen so many people in one place, even during the sheep dipping at the river, and his heart picked up the pace. There were men and women who must've come from other villages in the Hillakes, looking forward to an evening's entertainment and a slice of pie. Most of them wore homespun clothes made from the grey-brownish wool the regional sheep produced, but here and there Far spotted a scrap of red linen.

A group of young women had pushed the boat out and made garlands of primroses and daisies for their hair, loath to let any opportunity go by to impress a miller's son. They took a step back as Far approached; he was obviously not what they had in mind.

At last, he squeezed through into the taproom where the noise was deafening, laughter and the clatter of wooden plates and tankards, and then into the familiar smell of too many bodies squashed together. Far pulled the shiny leather pouch he had carried with him for the last months from his jacket and fished out one of the precious copperlings. The queue moved quickly, and he paid for the beer and two small loaves of bread, although he could smell the pies. His stomach rumbled. He used his bony shoulders to push the other patrons out of the way and found Cas sitting on a bucket at the edge of the yard, his face brightening as he took his tankard from Far.

"I can't remember it being this packed last year," the miller's son said, sipping.

Far gave him the bread, noticed the disappointment, and decided to ignore it. While he'd been inside, dusk had crept up and the first torches had been lit. A slow drumbeat started. The beer was cool and bitter, the bread fluffier than he was used to and lightly flavoured with pepper and cinnamon. He sighed happily. There weren't a lot of spices used in Sheepdip; in fact, he couldn't remember when he'd last tasted cinnamon. He tried to eat as slowly as he could, while Cas wolfed down his loaf in a few bites. Cas was used to better bread.

"Do you really want to stay back there?" Far asked. "You won't be able to see a thing." He couldn't help being a bit annoyed with Cas. They had planned the day for so long, the day when they would walk over the ridge to see the players, and now Cas was behaving as if he'd been dragged down against his will. Maybe his brothers had really got to him.

Cas brushed the crumbs off his fingers. "I'll find you later. Go on—you better get a move on if you want to get anywhere near the stage."

Far swallowed. He would've loved to see Cas watch the tale, to share the excitement of the unfolding story with him. Instead, Far stuffed the rest of the bread down his shirt to make his way through the crowd. The audience had become restless since the drum started playing; everyone tried to jostle for a better position, and he had to go past the garlanded maidens again, who suddenly had very sharp elbows. He tried to turn around but couldn't see Cas anymore—likely still sitting on his bucket and sulking that Far's budget hadn't been big enough for pies.

Far bit his lip, took another sip from his beer, and faced the stage. The barn door stood open, and a red cloth glistened in the light of the torches, moving slightly back and forth. A lute player stepped out into the sanded square.

Far's mouth went dry as the audience began to clap. They all looked forward to leaving winter behind and welcoming in spring, notoriously late in the Hillakes, and they cheered as the players walked onto the stage.

The bard introduced each of the characters as had always been the custom: the Cruel King, the Wicked Sprite, the Shepherd. The crowd held their breath for the Queen. The man who played her was gaunt and older than Far had pictured him, but his eyes were as blue as the bright spot in the middle of the Lightwater on a sunny day, and the horsehair wig was as red as a sunrise in the depth of winter.

Far's jealousy took him by surprise. He almost dropped his beer. His fingertips prickled as if he'd been pushed into the nettle patch again and his heart raced. Those players would ruin the story—there was simply no other way.

2
OFF THE ROAD

IF YOU DON'T SHUT up now, I'll have to drown you, Far." His eldest brother stood hip-deep in the river, brown hair plastered to his shoulders.

"But they really could've done it so much better! Thank Heavens it's a different play this time. I'm not sure if I would part with my money otherwise." The disappointment Far felt after wasting his coin on the performance still clung to him. With every line the Queen had uttered, his resentment had bubbled up like ale barm mixed into flour.

His brother groaned and closed his fists. The paddock gate clicked, and the next lot of sheep were released onto the gravel.

It had been a hot couple of days, but Far's teeth chattered as he approached the closest ewe, grabbed her by the fleece, and pulled her with him into the waters of the river. Dirt welled up from the struggling animal in thick brown clouds and was carried away by the current towards the village, which had once upon a time been given its name because of the natural basin formed by the river after it emerged from the hazel plantation at the edge of the woodland. Only this bit of the riverbank was shallow enough for the sheep to be herded through and washed before the annual shearing a few days later.

The ewe that Far grappled with was one of the older animals and had been dipped a few times in her life; she bucked and plunged deeper, determined to take him with her. Far stumbled and released his grip for a moment, and off she went, bleating triumphantly, to join her slightly cleaner sisters on the other side of the water. It wasn't the first dunking he'd received today, and it wouldn't be the last, but his muscles ached and his fingers spasmed as he tried to rub some warmth back into them.

"Your lips are turning blue." His brother, of the same height but bulkier, stronger, and still flushed from the struggle with the last lot, pointed a thumb behind him in the direction of the pens. "Go and get some tea," he ordered," and send a few of the others."

They took shifts in the dip, and Far was relieved his had ended early. He waded up the gravel bank. For the dipping, a double line of wattle hurdles had been erected from the gate of the pen to lead the sheep into the river. He had to walk up to the paddocks and climb over the fence.

The maze of pens held various groups of sheep, all at different stages. By the end of the process, every one of them would've been checked over, cut back at the hooves if necessary, dosed with a bitter-smelling herby concoction that was supposed to help with worms, counted, and finally released to be cleaned up as much as possible.

As he approached, a couple of other boys split from the group of men and dogs around the paddocks and made their way down to the dip. Apparently, no one had expected him to last particularly long. He knew he was supposed to feel ashamed, but his relief at being out of the freezing water was too strong. He pulled off his shirt as he went, wringing water from it in long ropes of brownish droplets that dripped into the cropped grass. The midday sun burned his naked back and would likely make him break out in the freckles that already covered his arms and shoulders.

A few cooking fires were kept going near the pens, with big pots of tea and stew bubbling away to warm up the dippers. One of the dairy maids of Riverbend handed him a wooden bowl.

The tea had been brewing for a good long while, and he wondered whether he'd been given the de-worming tincture by mistake, but tried to concentrate less on the revolting bitterness than on the warmth. His brother would've been offered something stronger, something alcoholic, and though Far had long been of the age where most boys developed a taste for the brandy that could be purchased in tiny bottles from the coach station, he'd only ever been allowed tea or small beer.

He tried to squeeze as much water as possible from his trousers, hung his shirt on a segment of the fence where the sheep wouldn't be able to get it, and slumped down in the sun, still shivering and covered in goosebumps. Everyone was expected to help, including someone the others kept away from, even the miller's boys who usually deemed themselves far above the shepherds.

Cas had been in the first shift at the river. Far hadn't spoken to him in weeks, not since they'd returned from their frustrating day at the play and Far had jerked him off behind the grain store. While Cas had seemed to enjoy that bit of their interaction, he freaked out as soon as Far tried to kiss him afterwards. Ever since then, no one had really come near him. Far's brothers seemed to have closed in on him in earnest, like dogs protecting a lamb from the wolves, although it had taken him weeks to persuade one of them to come with him to the next play tomorrow; in the end they'd drawn straws to decide who had to keep an eye on him and listen to him chatter all the way across the ridge.

Thinking about the future helped immensely. He finished his tea and flung the dregs over his shoulder into the grass. He would see the players again, albeit a different company, one that had come to kick off the Shortest Night celebrations in Halfway. The Shortest and Longest Nights were the highest feast days in the kingdom, and festivities began weeks before the actual events.

In the Hillakes, the dipping and shearing took place much later than in the southern lands, shortly before the hay was cut and everyone needed to be distracted from the back-breaking work that wouldn't stop until autumn, when early snow would dust the hilltops and the fleeces of the sheep had long since grown back to protect them from the changeable weather. The summers were short and never quite as warm as wished for, though Far's hair dried quickly, and he started to feel better.

He was thinking about asking for stew when he saw the brother who'd drawn the shortest straw coming towards him. His feet were as bare as Far's own, but he hadn't been in the water yet. He wasn't the eldest but the tallest. People said that Far looked most like him; they both had the freckles and the same wide brown eyes.

"You're clearly much happier here," his brother said, touching his clammy shoulder. He gave Far half a pie, filled with spring greens and some of the tangy cheese that Riverbend Farm was known for.

Far nodded and took a large bite. If he was very lucky, he might find a bit of mutton somewhere in the filling.

"Listen," his brother began, and disappointment nearly turned the food in Far's mouth to dust. "Would you be fine going on your own tomorrow?"

Far managed a shrug. At least he would still be allowed to go. Probably.

"Yilis wants to go to the fires and ...."

His brother had started going out with one of the dairy maids from Lightshore Farm a few months ago, and she wasn't known to pay much attention to anyone who crossed her plans. Far knew she wouldn't give his brother a choice now that everyone expected them to get married.

"It's fine," he lied, eating the rest of the bribe his brother had brought. He was used to being on his own. "As long as I can tell you about it when I come back."

His brother's smile flickered for a moment, but then he sighed. "Of course, Far."

"Would Yilis like to hear about it as well?" Far added maliciously, enjoying the hint of panic in his brother's voice.

"She's really not that interested in plays. She doesn't even like fairy tales. She ...."

"Breathe. I'm kidding."

His brother flushed. "Well played."

But rattling him didn't take away from the knowledge that Far would be on his own, would once again have no one to share his passion with.

Far awoke with a horribly stiff neck and to a chorus of snoring people who seemed to have collapsed around him in the night. He rolled up his bedding and had a quick wash before putting on the clothes he had purposely kept clean for the occasion. At least he was able to leave on his own terms, now that no one was coming with him; he didn't have to wake anyone.

Some of his sisters were already about, milking the cows and feeding the chickens. They gave a little wave as he walked up to the mill where Sheepdip Bridge crossed the river, where he stood for a moment to look towards the lake and the sun rising steadily over the eastern hills.

Perhaps he felt that he needed to remember that exact moment before he walked along the western bank of the river towards the woodlands, past the empty pens where some people still slept while others huddled around the fires, waiting for the first batch of tea. They nodded as he went past in his clean-ish boots and best jacket, his hair combed and bound back from his scrubbed face.

He passed by the dip and followed the path through the hazel into the oaks, beeches, and larches. The birds stopped singing as he came through the trees. He assumed he'd walk back the same way in the evening, and the muscles in his calves protested as he climbed towards the ridge.

The soil had dried up; he began to sweat and wiggled out of the jacket. He paused again once he reached the ridge and sat for a few heartbeats on a clump of grass. For once the slopes were almost empty, the sheep on the other side of the valley, kept closer to be at hand for shearing. A few ponies stood grouped around the gorse bushes and nibbled at their spiny branches. Beneath them, the Northwater glistened in flaming ripples. The Hillakes were beautiful and his heart beat in its rhythms. It was the first time that Far understood where he came from, even if he had always wanted to leave.

Smoke drifted up from the smithies at the coach station and the chimney of the bakery, spreading like a thin mist over the village of Halfway in the Hillakes. He saw the preparations for the bonfire, people carrying logs over the Great Road in a long line of handcarts. There would be many travellers on their way, trying to reach home and family for the feast days; it was the station's most profitable season of the year, and they had their own festivities, their own rituals.

When Far crossed the Eastbridge, he saw the three big wagons the players travelled in standing in a half circle on the shore of the Southwater. Washing lines had been drawn between them to air out the costumes. Someone was sitting by the fire.

Far didn't pause to think. He stepped off the road.

3
BOIL AND BUBBLE

T HE MAN WHO SAT on the wooden chest had a copper basin before him, a thin piece of soap, and an array of blades. He narrowed his eyes at the boy coming towards him.

"You don't look old enough to shave."

Far stopped a few paces from the fire, gritting his teeth as he readied himself to plunge into a new life. "I can help," he blurted out. "Not with shaving. I've worked on the farm all my life and am stronger than I look."

The man rolled his eyes. "Not another one," he rumbled. "We barely fit in the wagons as it is, boy."

"I can walk."

"Sure you can."

"I can ... I know stories."

Something changed in the barber's face. "Stories?"

"There are lots of local fairy tales, not just 'The Queen under the Lake'. Once upon a time there were many castles in the Hillakes, many strongholds. They're all gone now of course, but the stories were left behind, and I learnt them from my grandmother when she was still around, and I know other ones too, not just from here. Everyone likes stories of kings and knights and queens and the Wicked Folk, even the inklings in Seagard."

The barber kicked one of the dry logs next to the fire sideways so that Far could sit down.

Far looked at him in surprise. The man was clean-shaven and his slate-grey hair twisted into a long braid. Like Far, he was probably older than he seemed.

"Have you ever been to Seagard ...?"

"Faral. But everyone calls me Far."

"That's a weird name. Lucky for you, I like weird. And—have you been?"

"There's no way a shepherd from Sheepdip-on-Lightwater finds his way down to Seagard and back up again."

"Lightwater? As in 'The Queen under the Lake'? How far is that from here?"

"About three hours walk over the ridge, the next valley over."

"It's supposed to be beautiful."

Far thought about the view from Sheepdip Bridge. "Of course it's beautiful. The Hillakes are famous for being beautiful, from top to bottom."

"And the Queen's castle?"

"Some of the stones are left, but the site isn't easy to find. A few years ago, one of the inklings came to the village. Said he wanted to write a book. My brothers took him up to the castle, and in the end, he was really disappointed. We warned him before he made the trip, but he wasn't very good at listening."

"The inklings never are. They'd rather believe in books than in people." The man squinted at Far. "Can you read?"

Far squirmed. "A bit. Enough."

The barber's blue eyes narrowed again. "Can you write?"

"I can write my name. Sort of." Far pulled a pained grimace.

"Would you be willing to learn?" The barber studied Far's face and added, "All the men in this company can write and read, but no one calls us inklings, though in a way we make our living from it. Think about it—if you really want to come and help, it's one of our conditions. It's a useful skill to have and worth the trouble. Does your mother know you want to leave?"

Far nodded. All of them knew he would leave eventually. No one expected him to become one of the inklings, but maybe the barber was right. Maybe .... Blood burned in his face.

"You won't be paid," the barber warned him, leaning forward and pushing the waterpot deeper into the embers. "You won't be paid for a long time, but I assume you're used to that? Working for bread and a bed? We leave early tomorrow, moving on to Blacktowers. There won't be much time to say goodbye."

No time to say goodbye to his brothers and sisters. He swallowed his rising grief. No time to say good riddance to Cas. "Oh, I'm not going back home."

"You've never even seen us perform."

"I'm willing to risk it."

"Are you now?" The barber checked the water. "Still not hot enough. Piece of advice? At least ask for names. I don't think I've ever seen someone as desperate as you."

Far's stomach curdled with anticipation. Would he really be allowed to stay? "Right. What's your name?"

"Ravael, or Rav. I'm the man who plays the Knight." He shuddered. "Sometimes the Young King, if I really have to. Oh, and one time I had to be the Wise King, but we had to glue on the beard and my face was itchy for weeks afterwards. If you ever see them coming with the glue pot, run." He smiled as the water finally began to boil and bubble. "Tea?"

The smell of brewing herbs wafted over to the three wagons and prompted the next appearances. None of the men making their way to the fire gave Far a second glance. Maybe it was normal to find someone new sitting in their midst in the morning. Perhaps they assumed that someone had acquired a new friend during the night.

A young man with an unusually narrow face brought over a plate of cheese biscuits and a few cuts of cold meat, leftovers from an earlier meal in the coach station. Far wanted to grab a handful of slices but only took one piece. It was the most delicious thing he'd ever eaten, heavily spiced to the taste of the inklings and only slightly dry. The biscuits were nice as well, though the cheese was not as strong as he was used to.

The players wore woollen trousers and linen shirts because there was work to do in the mornings, but their faces matched the roles they would take on later in the day. The man with the narrow face surely was the Princess, and the one with the soft black eyes, the Prince; the Wise King had a beard and seemed very hungover. None of them had the face Far wanted for the Queen.

They shared their food and their tea with him but talked among themselves. A few sat down for a shave, and Rav used a brush to make foam from the soap and tested the blade on a leather strap. Others drifted to the fire and away again to the wagons. Still no one spoke to him until Rav flicked a bladeful of foam and bristles into the fire. Once the hissing flames had drawn everyone's attention, he said, "We have a new boy who plays the Page."

The whole company stared at Far.

"He looks ... unusual," said the dark-skinned man who played the Prince.

"Don't be mean. He could still run away again and then where would we be?" The man who surely played the Sorcerer, or the Evil Duke or the Devil, smiled at him and gave Far more tea. "Well done," he said quietly to Rav.

Far realized he was the youngest at the fire. If they were missing the Page for today's entertainment, he had been extraordinarily lucky. They needed him as much as he needed them. The Queen had to have a Page; the Knight had to have his Squire.

"He's taller than the other one," one of them said mournfully. "There might be some changes necessary."

"Make them," ordered the man who played the Wise King, rubbing his bloodshot eyes. "He doesn't need to talk in this one, does he?"

Rav gave a quick shake of the head. "There's the scene with the letter and the one with the cushion, when he brings in the magic ring at the end. Will you let Saran know?"

The Wise King looked even more uncomfortable. "Why me?"

"Because he won't yell at you. Probably. Did he drink as much as you?"

"I lost sight of him at some point. He took one of the girls back, that much I remember."

Rav sighed. "Of course he did. I hope this one isn't married. I still haven't recovered from the last time."

"At least he has his Page back." The Wise King turned to face Far directly. "Listen, boy. If you ever think of running away, just let us know a few weeks in advance. Travelling with the company isn't half as interesting as most people think and the work much harder than they expect. Leaving home to join the players is only the first step of many, and the adventure tastes much less sweet when you're digging your first of many shitholes for the camp."

Far nodded, his mouth too dry to speak. He had worked hard all his life. He forked muck from the farm's stables on most days.

Rav cleared his throat. "He says he's a shepherd."

"Can he read?"

"A bit."

"Can he write?"

"Not yet."

"Then you both have a few very busy weeks ahead of you." The Wise King gave the Knight a nasty grin.

Being the boy who played the Page began with trying to find a costume. At first Far was thoroughly embarrassed to stand in front of the first wagon in his smallclothes and struggle to fit into a variety of linen tunics and leather breeches. Most of them were too short, the other ones too big, but at long last a combination was found that worked for Rav and the man who took care of the costumes.

"Don't spill anything on it," they warned him before Rav made him put his old clothes back on, which felt rough against his skin.

"We're going up to the yard in a bit; you'll need to bring the costume, as most of our stuff is already in the barn. We set up the stage in the evening, so we'll have enough time for the run-through today before there are too many people about. Are you hungry?"

Far shrugged, then sighed and nodded. "I'm always hungry."

"The reason why we like to play in the stations is because they feed us well. Don't feel you have to hold back, but if you throw up on the stage, you're in deep shit. Same goes for beer. Don't drink before the performance. The apple juice is usually nice, and they use cinnamon in the one they have here. Beer and juice they often throw in for free, but we need to pay extra for the wine, so keep your hands off it if you don't want to end up washing dishes for half the night. I won't pay for you and nobody in the company will, either. If someone from the audience offers, best to avoid them until you're old enough to handle them. How old are you exactly?"

Far thought about lying but said, "As far as I know, I have eighteen summers to my name."

Rav blinked. "Oh. Sorry, you look a lot younger. I think it's the eyes."

"They're waiting for the face to catch up." Far sniffed, desperate not to give in to self-loathing. "At least that's what my mother says."

4
PROVE HIS WORTH

As soon as Far saw the man who played the Queen, he knew that he had no choice but to fall in love, which made Far hate him on the spot.

Saran was late for the run-through, in a long linen underdress held in with a loose-hanging tablet-woven belt. It made him look like a maiden from the old tales. His hair was flaming red and almost as long as the wigs the Queen usually wore, his shoulders surprisingly wide, his voice surprisingly deep. His face was beginning to soften around the edges but must've been devastatingly beautiful ten years ago. He looked as hungover as the Wise King, dark circles under his eyes and a bit green around the gills. He grabbed a bowl of strong tea from the trays the station's servants had brought into the barn and sank onto one of the costume chests, clutching the steaming vessel as if his life depended on it.

"Why?" Saran rasped as Rav took up the scene with the letter for the second time. "We've done this one so often, sometimes I dream about it. It's not one of your best, Rav."

The lines around Rav's mouth became more pronounced. "You've never tried writing one yourself," the Knight said through clenched teeth. "You're very welcome to. In case you haven't noticed, our company has a new member, and he hasn't done it before."

Saran's light brown eyes fell on Far. His glance travelled down, then back up, making Far's skin flush with discomfort and resentment. Saran shrugged. "He looks like a squirrel. Was he really the best you could do?"

"He'll grow into it. It's your fault the Page left in the first place. Get up. There's no time for any of your nonsense today."

The Knight turned away, and Far saw the smile that tugged at Saran's mouth. The man who played the Queen slid from the chest, downed his tea, and grabbed one of the folded cloths that had been prepared for the table where the players would later put on their faces. He wrapped it around his shoulders in a single fluid move, and with that gesture he changed into the Queen.

Saran was astonishing. Far had trouble keeping his eyes off him. Though Saran wasn't in costume and only spoke his lines for Far's sake, something in his voice pulled all the attention to him. The players were used to it, tried to ignore it, but from time to time Far caught the Prince staring at the man who played his mother-in-law.

The text was based on a story Far hadn't heard before that made use of all the characters. He realized this company was better than the ones he had seen before, even if the play itself wasn't particularly interesting. The man who played the Fool was magnificent, and Rav had given him the best lines.

They ran through Far's scenes a few times to make sure he knew what was expected of him, and then the company dispersed to eat, prepare the costumes, and put on the paint. Everyone seemed to have their own lengthy routines, and Far felt in the way after the man who played the lute had helped him smear more kohl around his eyes and dab some fat boiled with redroot on his lips. He would only be on stage for a couple of moments; though they *needed* the Page, they merely *accepted* his presence.

He found a bucket and sat down, watching the slow transformations happening around him in the barn. Each man seemed to slip into a different person. Suddenly they were alert and efficient; even Saran shrugged off the languidness as he enhanced his own beauty to match the role he would perform. There were ten of them, eight players and two musicians, not the largest company Far had seen performing. They fell into three groups that kept close to each other, one for each wagon they travelled in. Three separate families. Far couldn't see a place for himself; he'd have to prove his worth and help, as he'd promised.

He sat on his shaking hands. For the first time in his life, he wasn't hungry at all. He almost wished to be back in the sheep dip, in the freezing waters of the river, the youngest son who was always a bit useless, a bit annoying, and definitely not in love with the man who played the Queen.

The musicians were the first to go out on stage, to draw the audience closer to the square. Next to the curtain that hung from the door of the barn, the players formed a line in order of entrance: the Wise King, the Young King, the Knight, the Prince, the Evil King, the Fool, the Queen, the Princess, and the Page. It was the traditional line-up for a simple story that ended with the Prince getting married to the Princess; the Evil King being vanquished by the Young King, the Knight, and the magic ring; and the Wise King recovering from his mysterious illness— satisfying solutions for an audience that longed to drink and forget the gruelling weeks of the harvest that would follow the Shortest Night feast.

No one wanted to think about what was to come, and everybody craved to cheer when the Wise King rose from his deathbed, when the Prince finally kissed the Princess, when the Evil King burst into flames of red and yellow silk strips that were sewn to the inside of his long cape, dancing and flickering in the light of the torches when it was turned with an energetic *swoosh*.

Far heard them clapping, all the people who had come to see the players at Halfway coach station, as he himself had come for years. The characters went out to meet their audience one by one, until Far was the last one left in the barn.

He breathed in, breathed out, then pulled the curtain aside. The heat of the torches licked over his forehead and the tip of his nose. The Page received his share of expectant applause. On his side of the light, he only saw the first row of faces; the other spectators merged into one dark mass, like a lake in the darkest of nights. He paused, counted to eight as they had told him to, then he was the first one back in the barn. The others followed, the musicians changed the tune, and finally the play began.

"Next time you need to look at my shoes, not my face." Saran flicked his hair back and loosened the sleeves on the floor-length gown that was embroidered with a multitude of blue stars. He tossed the sleeves aside. "Heavens, I need a drink now. What's your name again? Far? You might want to think about changing that. At least you have a nice enough voice. Ask Rav to give you a few lines when we get to Blacktowers."

Saran unhooked the dress and shrugged it over his shoulders. He had almost as many freckles as Far. He swore into the rustling fabric before he managed to free himself, the skirts sliding over his head, so he was left standing in the reed-stiffened stays and the long underclothes he wore as an outer garment when he wasn't officially in costume.

He looked younger with his hair tousled and the kohl around his eyes smudged from the effort of undressing. It was the first time Far had the specific thought: *Maybe I could be him.*

Saran had a distinctive smell, which clung to all of his costumes, and as soon as he'd unlaced, taken off the stays, and put on his woven belt, he left the barn to find himself a beer and probably one of the garlanded women. Far picked up the sleeves, flattened them with his palms, and drew the dress from the floor onto the costume chests; the perfect excuse to breathe in the scent of woodsmoke and juniper berries, with a weird, sweet note that probably came from the cosmetics Saran had used earlier to give the Queen the face the audience expected. When Far looked up, he saw the man who played the Prince watching him.

"I only wanted to ...." he mumbled.

The Black man who played the Prince peeled off his silk jacket with the silver-painted buttons and smiled sadly. "You're not the first to fall for him. He'll use it against you, mark my words. I've played with four different companies, and usually they centre around the Kings, not the men who play the women. We wouldn't be here, we wouldn't be on our way to the southern lands, if it wasn't for him." He stretched out his hand and Far shook it. "Jom. I joined the company last year, after I saw them at the Harvest Festival in Eastbay. You already decided to come with us?"

Far managed to nod, but his mouth was dry.

"It's better in summer." Jom folded his jacket with care and changed the princely slippers for boots caked in dry mud. "You're probably in the same wagon as me; the last Page was. I'll show you what to do in the morning," he promised. "Now we should find something to eat. Come with me."

They left the barn together while the musicians took down the curtain and started packing up. The yard was still filled with people. Jom took his elbow, guiding him to the entrance of the taproom where one of the tables had been reserved for the company, already littered with breadcrumbs, half-drunken tankards, broken biscuits, and nutshells. There sat one of the big sheep milk cheeses with a knife sticking in the top, a plate of dried apples in honey, and butter glistening with salt crystals; there waited small, round cakes filled with something very sour and pungent that Far had never tasted before, and buns stuffed with almond paste. Next to the cheese stood a platter with slices of pie that had more meat than greens in the filling and baked eggs, the shells still grey with the warm ash they had cooked in.

"Slow down." Saran stood next to him. "If you're the first to puke, you lose." His pale face softened. "They give us so much food because they don't want to pay the price we asked, but still need us to come back next year. Jom, from now on, he's your responsibility."

The Prince sighed. "Figured as much."

"He'll help loading up in the morning, but he's probably never handled a proper horse before. If he snores, we'll ditch him in Blacktowers. Pass the wine jug." Saran noticed Jom rolling his eyes. "I've already paid for this one," the man who was queen snapped. He half threw himself over the table to reach the jug, almost knocking the sour cakes off the side.

As soon as his back was turned, Jom leaned towards Far and whispered, "Do you want to know why he's in such a mood? We're going to pick up his wife in Blacktowers."

5
OPINIONS

IT HAD STARTED TO rain in the night, which didn't help with the preparations to leave Halfway. Far spent his first night in the wagon he shared with Rav, Saran, and Jom. It was surprisingly roomy, with partitions for some privacy. The beds were made on top of the travel chests, all pushed together to form a single layer.

It felt strange to sleep with so many new people around, especially one he dearly wanted to kiss; he almost missed his brothers and thought for a while about what his family would say when they realized he wasn't coming back to the village. He thought about what Cas would think and hoped that he would start planning his own escape soon. Then Saran almost fell on him trying to get out for the third time, only to throw up very noisily next to the left front wheel.

When Jom woke Far in the morning, a thin mist lay on the Southwater, resisting the rain. They pulled halters from the box under the wagon and went in search of the horses, dew soaking through the bottoms of their trousers. Halfway Common stretched around the southern side of the village down to the edge of the lake, so they followed the curve of the Southwater. Cattle clustered around the shallowest bits where they were able to drink, some of them standing up to their bellies among the ripples the rain made on the surface. A quicker movement drew Far's eye; some animals were coming towards them. Among them walked the man who played the Princess, with three of the big draughthorses in tow, and behind him the man who played the flute, leading the other three.

"Thank you!" Jom ran towards them.

The Princess shook the wet fringe out of his eyes. "They were all the way down, almost next to the Westbridge." As he came near, Far saw that the third horse didn't wear a halter; the Princess held it with a piece of rope around its muscly neck that he released as soon as Jom reached them. Jom fastened the buckles and passed the rope attached to his halter to Far, then went to retrieve the next horse from the musician.

The Princess smiled at Far. "You look as if you know what you're doing."

"We have ponies on Riverbend Farm. I'm used to working with them."

"Definite advantage. The last Page had no idea when he joined, and I can't say that I miss him complaining. Why do you want to be a player?"

Far shrugged. "Probably better than being a shepherd in the Hillakes."

"Better in what way?"

"At least you get to see something else. Other lakes, other ... hills. I've never been to Blacktowers before. And you get to tell stories, every day, without anyone thinking you're weird."

Jom caught up to them and they started walking back to camp, the horses between them. Far touched the neck of the one he'd been given, felt the warm, dry coat underneath the shaggy mane. The horses smelled familiar. He knew that he'd learn how to handle them quickly; they were friendly and quiet and followed at the slightest pull of the rope. Someone had trained them well. They stood still while Jom showed Far how to put them in harness and hitch them to the wagon.

While they were gone, Rav had tidied up, made space for the chests they would collect from the barn, and rolled Saran into a corner where he wouldn't be in the way. Rav was the one who took the reins, and theirs was the first wagon ready to leave camp.

Far climbed up next to him. It was the first time he'd seen the Hillakes from a new perspective; suddenly Halfway seemed smaller and not as important. They loaded up the props and costumes, then collected provisions from the taproom. The Wise King was the one who was paid for the company's performance, probably because he was the oldest, the only one with a real beard. People just assumed he was in charge. When they returned to the wagons, Far pulled one of the stable boys aside, who had helped to hold the waiting horses.

"If someone comes and asks for Far, or maybe Faral, tell them I've joined the players and am going away with them."

The boy snorted, gave him a look clearer than anything he might've said to express his disgust. "There's always a stupid one."

Far rode up front next to Jom and Rav, while Saran slept in the back of the wagon; his heart raced ahead when they passed over the Westbridge. He'd seldom been further west in his life. Past Halfway there never seemed to be anything interesting before, only smaller settlements and then the next district. He'd never left the Hillakes, though he knew that Blacktowers was at the border and must've been important at one point, before the steady stream of travelling inklings had turned the stations into the valuable assets they were today. He was excited to finally be travelling himself, *actually* travelling, not just wishing he was somewhere else. Far away from the boys in the village who looked at him in a way that made his skin crawl, because Cas must've told someone that he'd tried to kiss him. He must have. Cas had never been good with secrets. And kissing was worse than touching. Kissing meant something.

At one point he turned around and tried to look back at the hills framing the valleys, at where he'd come from, but from the Great Road they were much less impressive, something that could be left behind without regrets.

Rav and Jom were used to travelling together and soon fell into one of those chats where the words weren't that important. Far couldn't really make sense of them. He stared down at the two horses, the nodding ears and the manes that fell down both sides of their necks, and he knew that until he'd proven his worth to the company, even the beasts had more status than him. He needed to make every moment count. He needed to learn, and for a moment the sheer thought of all that work made him freeze up.

"Something wrong?" The Knight watched him warily. "Already homesick?"

"No, just ...."

"Don't let him tease you." Jom briefly let his shoulder touch Far's. "It's a big deal to leave home, and all of us remember how it felt when we joined. I was scared shitless for a month, and the first company I played in didn't make it feel like the wisest of life choices. They were on their way down, and I jumped ship as soon as I could."

Rav cleared his throat, a warning that if Jom expected him to tell his own story, he was very much mistaken. Jom kicked his shin, and he yelped. "I can barely remember it!"

"Of course you can. I'm trying to make him feel better. Which play have you got in mind for Blacktowers, then?"

The Knight was visibly relieved at the subject change. "Maybe 'The Prince and the Toad'?"

"The Page doesn't talk in that one."

Far crossed his arms and held himself steady when he asked, "Do you have a version of 'The Queen under the Lake'?"

Jom looked nervous. "We had—at one point. But he hated it." He moved his shoulder back in a way that left no confusion about who had objected.

"What about 'The Fairy Knight'?" Rav asked. "He has a lot of good lines in that one, and the Page is almost always on the stage. I can find some words for him to say."

"Is that the one where the Knight travels through time to rescue both the Prince and the Princess?" Far asked.

Jom and Rav exchanged a quick glance. "Yes."

"I never really liked that story; it left too much unexplained. Why does time go by so slowly when he's underground? Why is the Fairy Mound bigger on the inside? Why is the Prince so stupid—it can't all be the inbreeding, surely?" Far caught them staring at him. "What? I said I like stories, and I know a lot of them."

"You obviously have quite strong opinions about them too," the Knight said quietly.

"Some just don't work," Far huffed.

"Apart from 'The Queen under the Lake', which ones are your favourites?" Jom asked.

"I like almost all the Pirate stories, and some of our local ones are good. Lots of enchanted castles, monsters hidden in the lakes, and mysterious lights in the water."

Jom's dark brow furrowed. "Lights in the water?"

"That's where the name of the lake comes from," Far explained. "I've never seen them, but my eldest brother swears he has, and of course everyone has their own theories about them." He could feel himself catching fire. "Some link them to the Queen and others to the waterhorses. I used to fear waterhorses when I was little, thinking they would travel upstream from Lightwater. Riverbend Farm was right next to the banks and our hut the closest. When I woke in the night, I always thought I'd hear something coming up from the water, crunching on the gravel, dripping on the grass." Far stopped and smiled.

"I have goosebumps," Jom complained. "Rav, you could do one about a waterhorse, couldn't you? We need something new for the Harvest Festival, and we could use it for the afternoon slots when we're in Seagard in early winter."

Far's breath caught in his throat. "Seagard? We're going to Seagard?" A whole city crammed full of inklings—so many people no one in Sheepdig wanted anything to do with—but also the port where most of the spices landed that trading companies shipped from all over the known world.

"Eventually," Rav said. "Saran was able to call in a few favours last year, and it worked out so well that we're doing it again. They have proper theatres down there, and it means that we can keep off the road for a bit and still get paid. It's not as profitable but sharing the theatre for a few weeks guarantees us a fixed fee. We still have to pay for stabling the horses."

"You've both been to Seagard? Is it very big?"

"It's big and expensive," Jom sniffed, "and you have to keep all the inklings off you. They're so bored that they'll buy out every performance, especially when it's snowing and they want to get out of the cold."

"I'm going to be in Seagard ...." Far's mouth felt as if he'd tried to eat cold ash from the fire pits. He didn't feel ready to think about that kind of future.

6
THINGS CIVILIZED

Blacktowers had once been much larger, almost a town, before it burned down, all but the three watchtowers standing a quick walk away from the centre of the settlement. They were flame-scorched, crumbly, and reminded Far of rotten teeth.

The villagers mostly ignored them, saw them as the background to more important problems, but Far couldn't help but imagine how the night of the fire must've been for their ancestors, when the border had still belonged to a different kingdom and similar settlements were built around it to defend the Hillakes against the South.

It had taken them four days to reach Blacktowers. The wagons were slow, and Far learnt the rhythms of preparing the camp, what had to be done and when. Each afternoon the Wise King in the front wagon decided where to stop, and the horses were always Far's prime concern. At first Jom had helped, but after the first two days Far did it alone.

Rav preferred to do the cooking for the company, Jom built the fire and made the beds in the wagon, and Saran spent most of his days sleeping. No one expected him to lift a finger, but from time to time he joined in voluntarily, which always made Far very, very nervous. He couldn't wait for the next part of the evening to begin, when they would go through the scenes they planned to perform. They rehearsed between the fires. Because Saran was a wonderful Queen, Far was able to forgive him for all the things he'd said before he transformed. Far had his first lessons. Rav gave him a piece of slate and letters to practise, and although he hated the noise the iron-hard pen made on the stone, it was something to do while the wagons rumbled towards the border.

When they made camp in Blacktowers, he pushed the slate under the driver's bench and jumped off to start the preparations. He'd promised to work hard, and he did. The spot the Wise King picked for the stage was right next to the Northtower, in a space where remnants of the dwelling that once burned to the ground still stuck out of the grass. It formed a series of rooms that had housed the noblemen stationed to guard the settlement and their own families. Now their horses would graze among the ruins, and he would dig the latrines a bit further away.

In the last days he'd almost forgotten how it had felt to be on the stage in Halfway, and though he knew all his lines by heart, he was aware that it was possible for his mind to freeze in the moment, which would make Saran despise him even more. Not just because Saran found fault with the way he did *anything*, but because he'd realize Far was useless as a player. Saran would then use the influence he had over the others to kick Far out of the company because his handwriting was awful and sometimes he had problems remembering the shapes of the letters. The screeching of the pen on the slate echoed in the thoughts he had about himself. These worries only quietened when Rav asked him another question about waterhorses or the lights in the lake.

The Northtower was empty. No one seemed interested in living in such a spooky place. When Far stepped through the splintered doorframe after he'd finished with the horses, he understood why. Outside it was summer, almost the Shortest Night of the year, but within the blackened walls, the air felt icy. All the floors had burned away, as well as the roof, and a circle of light fell onto his boots.

For a moment he almost wished to be back in Sheepdip where something so eerie would never have been allowed to exist. In Sheepdip, the towers would've been utilized, made to serve as grain stores or stables. He touched the wall and turned around.

When he walked back into the camp, a woman stood next to the fires. She looked strong. Her clothes were those of the villagers, a dress made from unbleached linen and a grubby apron. Her hair was bound up with a yellow scarf, but her eyebrows were dark and almost met in the middle. "Another new Page?"

"The old one ran away," Rav said.

"Whose fault was that?"

"Do you need to ask?"

She grinned and nodded. "He looks nice," she decided. Far couldn't remember when those words had ever been said about him.

"Can he write?" the woman asked.

"He's getting there. He's a quick learner. Far, this is Malis. She's going to come with us, at least for a while."

"Nice to meet you," Far said. "Why were you in Blacktowers?"

"My mother lives here. I come and visit when I can."

Rav made a sympathetic face. "How is she?"

"Worse, as expected. My sisters are doing their best to keep her comfortable. I assume he's still sleeping?"

Rav shrugged. "The drinking started again."

"It always does. He hates coming here." Malis made an odd movement, a gesture that expressed annoyance, anger maybe, or exhaustion. "I'll try to keep things civilized," she promised.

To Far's amazement, Malis did not join his own wagon crew. She stayed with the Wise King, the Young King, and the Princess, and kept out of the way until the evening, when Saran stuck his head out of the covers, looked around, and proceeded to appear in his usual getup.

He whispered to Rav, "Is she here yet?" and received a stony-faced nod.

Saran looked apprehensive, a mood Far had never seen him in before and which almost made Far like him a bit. It was good to know there were things on Earth that made even the Queen so anxious that he kept fiddling with his hair.

Malis joined them during the first run-through in Blacktowers. Rav and the Wise King eventually decided on "The King in the Clouds," because the Queen had a smaller part than usual but still some of the best scenes. There was no Knight in it, and Rav had to play the Third King. Considering how he detested the glue-on beard, Far was aware that he saw his choice as a sacrifice to keep the company happy. The Prince did all the saving in that one, and Far loved watching Jom play such a big part. Far was his Squire and with him all the time. He even changed costumes twice.

Malis came up to the fire when they were halfway through, sat on one of the chests, and watched silently, her face unmoved, even when the Prince was almost killed by the Evil Duke and only made it because he kept a fat bunch of his father's letters close to his heart. This was the bit in the story Far had always loved, and he resented her for watching without any reaction whatsoever. She might've seen them perform the twist a dozen times or more, but it was still a good scene. Maybe this was why her marriage was in such trouble that she'd chosen to live in a different wagon and let Saran go off on his own.

As usual, they repeated the tricky bits, and then the musicians practised a few melodies while Rav prepared the evening meal. Saran and Malis went off together towards the Northtower, but they didn't talk while Far could still see them. He should've been jealous of the attention Malis received, but somehow his fascination for Saran included her too.

Rav noticed him noticing. The Knight stirred the stew and kept his eyes on the pot when he said, "They've been married a long time and have their own ways of communicating. We try to keep out of it."

"Are any of the others married?"

Rav nodded. "At one point or another. But usually, their wives prefer not to travel with us. Malis is the only one who joins us sometimes. She knows he needs a good bollocking now and then. We're always too soft on him."

"He looked afraid when he saw her."

"Because he knows what he's done. Don't worry about it, she knows it too. He always makes bad choices when he drinks, and he usually drinks. At the moment, she's with the Princess, but she's still keeping an eye on him."

"It's never so complicated in the stories," Far complained.

"Not in the ones people want to come and see," Rav said. "Get the bowls, Far; this looks ready to eat."

Far couldn't sleep. Perhaps it was because he'd perform as the Squire for the first time the next day, but his thoughts spiralled around the Queen. If not even Malis could keep Saran away from the wine, would Far be strong enough to keep caring for him? It didn't help that Saran slept only a few feet away. It would've been the easiest thing in the world to slide over, peel the blanket off him, and ....

When the first light crept into the wagon, Far shuffled to the back, opened the cover, and slid to the ground, his boots clutched in his left hand. It was very early, the sun barely up. His whole body ached, and his eyes seemed full of hot sand. He checked on the horses that grazed around the base of the tower; they came up to him, greeting him with their soft noses. It was almost enough to have their affection, but he couldn't shake off the wish to touch someone, to let himself be touched, even now that he knew it could never be the Queen.

Somehow, he made it through the morning's chores, then helped prepare the stage. People from the village built their own tents around the bonfire area. There would be whole pigs roasted on spits, spiced apple juice and cider, beer flavoured with herbs, elderflower wine, and lots of other goods for sale: baskets, medicines, necklaces, locks and keys, hats, chickens, ham, pickled onions, dried apples and mushrooms, cloth and ribbons. It was the biggest fair in the region, and people came from far and wide because it was one of the earliest.

Far and Jom found the flyers for the play and stuck them to anything that stood still, so "The King in the Clouds" would be advertised wherever people turned to look. Two performances were planned for each of the two days of the fair. Lots of spectators came to the first one in the afternoon, when the celebrations had just about started.

The Squire's costume had been adjusted to fit, but Far's collar tightened with every heartbeat. He hated the hours of waiting before he could step out for the first time, before he was called onto the stage so the whole village would know who he was.

There was the usual cheer when the musicians started to play and the Wise King strode through the curtain, followed by the Young King, the Third King and the Evil Duke, the Queen, the Princess, the Fool (who was a Nurse that day), and finally the Prince and the Squire. The audience knew the story, and the applause that greeted Jom and Far was deafening. Even Malis, who stood in the first row, smiled at them.

7
THE DARKNESS THAT LIVED

Y OU WERE REALLY GOOD." Malis gave Far a mug filled with chilled apple juice. "When the Prince came back to life, you looked as if you were over the moon with joy."

"Because I knew we were close to the end."

"Well, you used the feeling to great effect."

"Do you think anyone noticed I had the jacket on inside-out after the last costume change?"

"Who cares? Next time you'll know to check." She'd switched her yellow headscarf for a blue one and wore a clean blue linen apron; everyone had donned their best clothes for the summer fair.

Far sipped the cool juice, his throat stinging a bit. He had to be careful not to strain his voice too much; he only had a few hours to recover before they repeated the play for the next lot of spectators. He needed to eat, to touch up the kohl around his eyes, and get back into his first set of clothes.

With all the excitement of the first day, he hadn't practised his letters in a while, and he felt weirdly bad about it, as if he missed the piece of slate, was already half-addicted to the pen, when he should've rejoiced that he'd managed to remember his lines. Apart from the wardrobe mishap, everything had gone smoothly. The people loved the valiant Prince, the impertinent Nurse, and even the three squabbling Kings had received a few laughs. After the Evil Duke had been forced to revoke the curse and the Castle had returned from the clouds, Far felt as if he'd been part of the events, not just someone pretending. Maybe that was why he felt so drained, tired enough to ignore that he was quite hungry.

That Malis was nice about the whole thing helped. She took him by the shoulder and turned him towards one of the stalls, where he was promptly recognized as one of the players and given half a loaf of honey-sweetened bread filled with chopped nuts and apple butter. As soon as he swallowed the last mouthful, his head started to clear.

He had to go through the whole thing again, be the same kind of person, have the Squire's open face and innocence, the same love for his Prince. For the first time, he realized the ordeal that they went through performance after performance. It was painful to jump in and out. Perhaps that was why they were happy to be referred to by their roles. The Princess could keep on being the Princess, even when he brushed down the horses after a long day on the road, and the Fool, who was sometimes a Nurse and sometimes a Bear, kept the respect of the stage when washing out the stew pot at the end of the day.

Malis took him in hand, made sure he finished his juice and didn't wander off, the same things she must've done for her husband when he was new to the whole thing and unable to wrap his head around the possibilities his life could now afford him. When the musicians started playing again to draw in the crowd, Far was exactly where he was supposed to be, in his first costume, with his makeup fixed and his hair combed.

The second time around, he managed the costume change without getting into a panic and half-strangling himself with the knitted grey monstrosity that stood in for the Squire's mail shirt. Even Saran gave him a pat on the back afterwards, before squirming out of his own costume to proceed to the cider stalls. Far's heart violently skipped a beat. His feelings for the Queen were as complicated as ever, now that his wife had been kind. Suddenly his hunger came back; when the Young King brought a platter of roast pork and a basket of bread and sweet buns, the company gathered and celebrated—without Saran. No one commented on his absence.

They kept an eye on him, so Far made a point of only having a bit of cider, then switching to cold tea.

He went early to bed to be prepared for the next day of performances, though he had trouble getting to sleep with the noises of the fair in the distance. He woke up when the others came back to the wagon, felt Jom settle next to him on the straw-stuffed mattress. When he awoke again at sunrise, Saran still hadn't joined them. He'd clearly found some woman in the village who admired him enough to take him to her bed. Far couldn't help the bitter sting he felt, maybe on Malis's behalf, or because he still thought about the Queen in that way.

Far fell back into the routine of the camp: he fed the horses, checked the latrines, cleaned boots, and then got one of the fires going to make tea. He felt restless. The cool air of the morning stung his skin. He wondered if anyone else would be up for breakfast, anyone he could talk to, to avoid thinking about the Queen sleeping in a strange bed.

There was no reason to love Saran. He was rude, selfish, disloyal, hateful, and sometimes downright disgusting, but then he changed personalities coming onto the stage, and the light of the torches glinted off his hair and his face looked so different, capable of expressing the deepest of feelings: the Queen's ambition, the Queen's grief, the Queen's regret, and the love she felt for her daughter, her son, or her husband. He had all that in him. Perhaps he used up every last bit for the Queen so he couldn't keep anything back for himself, and that was why he burned brighter than the other players and made Far long for the same intensity, the same abilities. Far poked the logs in the fire, bringing them closer together. Finally they burst into flames.

"You're early again."

He looked up.

The man who played the lute, the one called Per, stood barefoot in the short grass, his dark hair rumpled and his linen shirt untucked. "Is there tea?"

"Not yet, but soon."

Per sighed contentedly, used his right foot to turn over one of the logs, and sat down. "You had a very good first day," he said after a few quiet moments. "They won't all be like this. Sometimes the crowd is hard to please. There were a few villages we had to leave in a hurry, though in Blacktowers people tend to be happy that we made the long way in the first place. It's different in the southern lands and *very* different in Seagard. In Seagard everyone needs to step up their game, even the Queen."

"Where is he?" Far cringed at the sound of his own voice.

Per must have noticed the desperation. "He'll be passed out behind one of the stalls."

"Should we try to find him?"

"He doesn't respond well to being rescued, as his wife will tell you."

"But ...." The water started to boil, and Far was grateful for the timely interruption. He scooped a handful of herbs out of the wooden box, put them into the teapot, and poured the water over, while Per fished two bowls from the kitchen chest. As he stood one of them next to Far, he lowered his voice. "He's used to people falling in love with him; they do it all the time. Then they try to get close to him for a bit, until they realize it's not him they want. They want what he can do, what he can make them feel."

Far's face burned.

Per smiled sadly, then touched his shoulder. "I think it's probably ready. I prefer it not too strong."

Far filled their tea bowls slowly to keep the leaves from floating through the spout. The tea had a very light colour but the bitter flavour that Far had come to expect. They sat by the fire, sipping.

Per cleared his throat. "Do you have your heart set on him?"

Far shrugged. He felt helpless, as if he'd already lost all dignity.

Per drew in a deep breath. "You can try, but no one is expecting a happy ending if you do. There are other ... options. You know that you need to be careful, especially when we cross into the southern lands?"

Far frowned. "What other options?" He stared up into the man's handsome face.

Per smiled, his eyes lighting up. "I hoped that bit would get your attention."

Whatever it was, it started on his second day in Blacktowers, after the last performance and after they made the first preparations for their morning departure. The costumes were all neatly folded, the chests with the props pushed under the wagons, the torches piled into a big heap, and the only reminder of where the stage had been was a square in the grass that wasn't trampled to mud like the rest of the field.

While the others sat down to drink, Far took Per by the wrist and pulled him to the Northtower. It was almost dark and woodsmoke hung over the camp. It was a relief to know Per didn't expect him to talk again; they made no promises before Far kissed him, because he loved the Queen and Per probably loved someone else. The darkness that lived in the tower was what they both wanted and had thought about during the day's performances, from the moment when Far first heard Per's musical introduction to "The King in the Clouds" and caught his eye with a quick private smile.

Per was closer to him in age and his eyes were a darker, warmer brown. Far would've noticed him much earlier if he'd known Per was interested, if he'd known that Per had done it quite a few times and there would be no horrible moment, no regret like when he'd realized Cas was quite happy to let him touch as long as there was no hint of tenderness, just functional movement.

Per allowed him as many kisses as he needed and asked if Far was fine as he gasped for breath because Per's hand was warmer than expected, with long nails that caught at his skin. In the end it only took a few moments, and they hadn't even removed all their clothes, but it was nice, and afterwards they laughed and kissed some more.

When they made their way back to camp, the Queen sat next to Rav at the fire with a big black eye, a split lip, bloody knuckles, and his own story to tell.

8
SMALL MERCIES

RAV EXPLAINED LATER THAT it happened sometimes, the occasional jealous husband or fiancé who underestimated the man who played the Queen and tried to take him on, but this one had apprenticed to the Blacktowers smith and was more than capable of standing his ground. Far heard the company laughing about it, but with a certain nervousness, as if the fights Saran got into often caused trouble for all of them.

Far studied Malis's face while her husband told the story, grinning from ear to ear, his teeth bloody. There was a hard line between her eyebrows, carved deep into her skin. She must've heard it a hundred times and long since stopped finding it funny. She clearly knew, as well as Far, that he sought these confrontations when he felt bad about himself, and that he'd deliberately picked the last day of the company's engagement so the swelling could go down before he put paint on his face again. Then it was easier to stay away from the beer and the cider because the pain gave him something to think about.

Far knew, because he'd played similar games with the boys in Sheepdip, although it seldom came to blows. For him, it had been suspicious looks and mean words. No one really wanted to touch him, and if push came to shove, his brothers still looked out for him, though they might get a few snide remarks themselves. The company ran on the same principles, and they were happy to close ranks around their best player, until one day .... Malis must've lived in fear of that. She must've felt the same urge for a long time, to finally leave him behind, to renounce him, because sometimes Saran was just so stupid and careless.

Far felt irrational guilt. He had gone off with Per to forget the Queen, and now Saran had been hurt, his hair hanging in long greasy ropes down his back as he tried to shake off the effects of the last jug of elderflower wine. Maybe it happened because Far took his eyes off Saran, found someone else for a few blessed moments.

He left the fires to crawl under his blankets, still hungry. His sleep was troubled, and he was relieved they had an early start. The company planned to cross into the next district and travel into the Southwest, to the Great Woods, where a noble family would hold their own festivities to celebrate both Shortest Night and the wedding of their eldest daughter. The family was able to pay for three whole days of performances, an old custom in the West.

Far did his chores as always, then Jom helped him hitch the horses to their wagon. When Rav was busy shaving the Fool, Jom took him aside. "Don't worry too much. He'll be a bit friendlier for a few days, and then everything'll start up again. He never really lets it get out of hand. He's too clever for that."

"I know why he does it."

"We all do. Rav asked me to give you a few more words to practise on the slate. We have a long way to go. The roads may be dry at this time of year but with the wagons it's difficult to take any shortcuts."

"Have you been there before?"

"Not with this particular family. With others in the district. Usually, it's a welcome break and almost on our way. Have you been to many weddings?"

"Not recently. One of my brothers is engaged to ...." Far's voice faltered. That was one wedding he'd have to miss. "What happens if he isn't well enough to perform?"

Jom smiled. "As I said, he's too clever for that."

"What if?" What if Saran was killed one day?

"The Princess will play the Queen. That's how it usually goes. When the Wise King dies, the Young King will step up. When the Queen ... dies ... the Princess will take on her new character. There are rules for every eventuality."

"Where does the Squire go, if …?" If he got the chance to stick it out with them.

Jom laughed. "That depends on the Squire. Rav wants to try out his new play in a few days. He's almost finished."

Far blinked in surprise. "But I haven't seen him write."

"He composes in secret. He hates it when we pester him about his progress. But he writes fast. You need to look at his hands; most mornings they're covered in ink. Not too long and you yourself will be able to …." He stopped, noticing Far's stare. "What?"

"I hadn't planned to become like them," Far whispered.

"Like them?"

"The inklings."

"I had a tutor when I was just a few years old. I was supposed to take over my father's business one day, until I decided I'd rather live a bit more dangerously. I have always been one of them."

Far's skin tingled with shame. "I didn't know."

Jom gave him a pat on the shoulder. "You're far from your village and soon we'll leave the Hillakes behind us. Where's the slate?"

There was a stone on the border, covered in moss. Far was able to read a few of the letters that were carved into it a long time ago, and all the numbers. Sheepdip-on-Lightwater had long ceased being important enough to be featured on the way stones. Far jumped off the wagon and walked across the border, almost expecting the road to feel different under the soles of his boots.

He lifted his gaze and saw Rav and Jom smile. Then Per caught up with him, took his elbow, and they walked a few steps together. The sun shone, and amidst the smell of the grass and flowers by the wayside, it felt like the best thing in the world to have a destination and a new play to learn the lines for. Far knew he shouldn't, but he turned around and, just for a moment, took Per into his arms and kissed him on the neck. He was happy and forgot that anyone might be watching.

No one said anything about it.

They made camp for the evening in a grassy hollow a few paces from the roadside. Dusk slowly fell over the trees that stood on the edge of the field behind them, a lazy sinking of the light. They felt the milder air of the summer night and for once there was no stew for dinner, but flatbreads baked in bacon fat, filled with cheese and some greens the Princess had collected when they brought the horses down to the narrow stream to drink.

The Knight sent Jom and the Fool to do the washing up but asked Far to stay behind. Something flickered in the light brown eyes of the Queen, a brief mirroring of the flames that painted out his bruises that had darkened during the day, but he didn't say anything either. Saran took another careful bite of his rolled up bread and leant back. Maybe he hoped Rav would forget about him.

The Knight pulled a bundle of papers from the satchel lying at his side and passed them to Far.

Some of the ink was smudged and Rav's writing hard to read. "I finished it. The Sorcerer will be the Waterhorse, and the Queen will be the Fairy from the Hill. We'll mix it up a bit for this one, make it a bit more ... unexpected."

"Why can't the Princess be the Fairy?" Saran's deep voice was very quiet.

"Because you would complain about him having the better part. I wrote it for you." Rav gave him a tight smile. "You should read it before you refuse."

"I don't like it when you change things around," Saran said. "It confuses the audience. The villain should be easy to identify, and you never know where you are with fairies."

"Well, that's the twist. It's interesting, because it's complicated."

"It's a weird story that nobody knows." There was something decidedly steely in Saran's voice now.

Far's heart broke into a gallop.

"It's your decision, but if we give the part to someone else, you won't get it back. Anyone would jump at the chance—even our newest member. Would you play the Fairy from the Hill, Far?"

Far could only nod; Saran's narrowed gaze didn't allow him to speak. A strange kind of hunger rose in his heart, ambition and delight to get his teeth into something new.

Rav smiled. "There you have it."

"I'll decide after the read-through," Saran said.

"Thank the Heavens for small mercies." Rav turned to Far so that his back was to the Queen.

Saran rose to his feet, tossed the rest of his bread into the fire, and left them to it.

"I want the Waterhorse to be so obviously evil that they don't suspect the Fairy, and when she finally reveals ...." Rav's face was flushed. "They'll all believe that the Prince is the one coming to the rescue, and the Princess—what?"

"You changed it?" Far cried.

"Do you disagree?"

"No, I think it's a good idea to keep them guessing. And if no one knows the original, no one will complain."

"Are there more stories about waterhorses?" Rav asked. "We could do a sequel if it's a success."

Far felt himself smile. "I could just make them up. How many lines does the Page have?"

"If you don't end up playing the Fairy from the Hill, you'll still have a good part, the Servant from the Hill. You'll even have a joke."

"Thank you," Far said, tears rising to his eyes. Perhaps he truly had worked hard enough to earn such recognition.

"I'm going to separate the parts tomorrow, but you can read some of it if you want. Let me know if you think I should change something else. No one has seen it yet; there's still time to switch stuff around."

Far touched the paper, cool under his fingertips. It felt strange to be trusted in such a way. He tried to flatten it against his knee.

The play was connected to him because he'd provided the bones of the story, because he'd loved his grandmother's tales about the waterhorses in the lakes that kidnapped the occasional farmer's daughter, or gullible shepherd's boy foraging for mushrooms in the fields, or sometimes even a pretty prince. They were shapeshifters and dangerous, and perhaps it had fascinated him as much as it fascinated Rav now, because everyone in the company had something of the waterhorse about them. Maybe even Malis.

9
A WORLD APART

THE GREAT WOODS IN the West felt disturbingly familiar. They were exactly how Far imagined the Enchanted Forests that featured in many of the tales. As soon as they entered the gloomy vales, he knew any play with fairies would be well received in this district. The creaking of the branches overhead and the rustling of the wind in the dry leaves next to the road made his hair stand on end.

The manor house they would spend the best part of the next week at was surrounded by a ring of gnarly oaks and smaller than Far had expected. It looked as if it had started out as a farm and been extended over several hundred years, its timber frame buildings in various stages of disrepair, though the main house had been recently re-thatched and painted a deep oxblood red, which made it stand out among the shabbier stables, workshops, and storage buildings.

Rav and the Wise King left the wagons to enquire in the yard.

Jom seemed nervous. He busied himself with tidying up the interior of their wagon while Far held the horses. Saran slipped from the seat at the front and shuddered into his linen dress, though it was a warm day.

"This house gives me the shivers." Saran brushed a strand of bright red hair behind his ear. "Why would anyone want to marry here? The last time we came to the Great Woods we played 'The Prince and the Toad' and I had the most horrible cold."

Since Rav had threatened the Queen might lose his bespoke part to Far, Saran paid more attention to the Page. It should've been exactly what Far wanted, but for some reason it added to the unease he felt in the woods. As expected, Saran had reconsidered as soon as he actually read the role that Rav had prepared for him, but it felt weird to have come between the Knight and the Queen. That Saran chose to talk to him now told Far he had to watch out. Even if what Jom had said was true and there were fixed rules on how the characters were awarded to the players, Saran was keeping an eye on him. That Far could be so much of a threat to the Queen was remarkable.

Saran crossed his arms when he stood next to Far. "Did I ever tell you how Rav and I met for the first time?"

Far shook his head. His hands, holding the reins of the horses, began to sweat.

"We've known each other for a very long time. I understand why he thinks he can use you against me. I started out as the Princess, as is proper. Rav poached me from another company, because he had something in mind for me. Doubtless he feels the same way about you. I'm not sure why." Saran smiled, and for the first time, anger towards the Queen kindled in Far.

During the previous days, the bruises had faded, and Saran would be back to his old form when they performed at the wedding. He would be the creepiest Fairy from the Hill that Rav could ever have imagined.

"There's a queue," Saran hissed under his breath. "They'll make Rav follow the rules, whatever happens. He knows that. He wouldn't dare push you to the front."

Far gulped and smiled back. "I'm not important enough for you to intimidate. I've only done two plays and only one with lines."

Saran's eyes glittered. "He likes you, and that makes you important. Don't underestimate the power of the man who writes the plays." Saran touched his shoulder, and his fingers burned through Far's sleeve. "You're not the first, and you won't be the last."

During the night the weather turned, and Far was woken by heavy raindrops drumming on the cover of their wagon; not the best omen for a midsummer wedding. At least there was space for them to perform indoors on this occasion.

The Wise King had explained their schedule for the next three days; they'd picked a few options with the father of the bride and would spend most of their first day in rehearsals to refresh their memories of "The Green Prince" and "Two Princesses, Swapped," both favourites of the family and thankfully staples in the summer repertoire.

Far had seen "Two Princesses, Swapped" three years ago at the Halfway station and knew that it usually required the Page to stand in for one of the royal sisters in the scenes when both Princesses had to be on stage at the same time. He had also seen Saran's face as the selection was announced. The Queen would try to keep Far as far away from a dress as possible. There were sure to be discussions as soon as everyone had received their first bowl of tea.

Far folded his hands and listened to the rain until he heard Jom move around under his blankets, yawn, and search for his shoes. Far sat up, and the Prince asked him with a gesture to follow him out of the wagon.

There was no space in the house for them, so the company had made camp between the oaks, but they were to be fed in the manor kitchen, which at least meant no cooking and no cleaning dishes. They wrapped themselves in their cloaks and ran to the gates of the yard. The kitchen was in a separate building next to the main house and had a staff room where long tables were set with plates piled high with fresh rolls and spiced buns, butter, cheese, and stewed fruit.

Malis and the Young King had arrived before them and the tea was ready. Malis patted the bench next to herself. "Come here, Far. I should speak to you before the yelling starts." She waited until he settled. "I noticed him talking to you yesterday. It's been a long time since I've seen him like that. What did you say to him?"

Far shrugged, suddenly annoyed that the Queen had so many people to fight in his corner. "I only tried to calm him down," he lied.

She grinned. "He's good at the game and knows when he needs to pull his finger out. I haven't seen him this sober for a while. It might actually help him."

A few days ago, Far would've been flattered. Now he scowled. "Whatever he thinks of me, surely I'm in no position to be dangerous to him."

"Yet," she said flatly before refilling her tea bowl. "He has enough of an imagination to predict where you might end up. Rav likes you because you understand him better than any of us. You're the one he chose to talk to about the new play. It's a very powerful position to be in, in case you haven't realized. Be careful around Saran, but don't let him scare you. If you're worried, I'm here to step in." She pulled a plate of warm currant buns towards them.

Far's stomach gave a loud growl, and she laughed, but Far knew his hunger did not only concern the magnificent breakfast. Being a threat to the Queen meant getting his attention, and it felt interesting, like a weird dance they'd started in the Great Woods of the West.

Malis ate quickly and left the kitchen to make space for the rest of the company who came in from the rain, one by one. The Princess sat next to Far on the bench. He reached for the buns, broke one of them apart, and wrapped it around a slab of cheese. "Are you sure you want to do it?" he asked between bites.

Far didn't have to check what he meant. If he stood in for the evil twin sister, he was setting himself up to follow the Princess. He sipped his tea that had almost gone cold. For a moment his stomach fluttered, then he gave a short nod.

The Princess swallowed. "Then we'll look at the costumes. We might have to make a few adjustments, and we need to find the wig. It's bound to be in the chest at the bottom of the pile."

Every one of them prepared for the inevitable confrontation. Far assumed that was how they kept themselves entertained during the touring months. He followed the Princess back to the wagons.

Most of the costumes were transported by Per's group, and he helped unearth them. They had put up a large, waxed linen tarpaulin between the vehicles so they could unpack the dresses and keep them dry. "Two Princesses, Swapped" required many versions of the same costume, and the one that Far was to wear was a little bit short and a little bit wide in the shoulders, but the blond horsehair wig fit like a glove.

The Princess plaited the hair back from his face. "I can work with this. I'll show you how to move. You'll only be on stage for a few moments, but it needs to be believable." He scratched the tip of his nose. "In a way, I look forward to seeing him angry. I wonder if that's really as wrong as it feels."

They started the celebrations off with the classics. Far had expected more people, but it was only a small wedding party. The eldest daughter was the last of them to get married, the relief on her parents' faces so visible that Far felt bad for her.

She was nice to look at, her hair hidden under the long cream-coloured veil, but her eyebrows were pale, and her face looked naked. That she had chosen "The Green Prince" and "Two Princesses, Swapped," both plays with more complex characters, meant she knew about stories. She might even have been taught to read and possibly had a very different life if she'd been brought up in the city, not in the middle of the woods where few people came by.

Her groom was less interested in the plays, but he seemed friendly. Far hoped that he would make a good husband for her. He hadn't expected to relate so much to the bride, but it allowed him to turn his gaze away from the Queen.

Per and the man who played the flute joined the musicians already at the manor. One of the bride's cousins had a wonderful singing voice, which added a different element to the performances.

They played indoors in the Great Hall of the manor that had been decorated with flowers and beeswax candles. Far had never seen a ceiling so high; the blackened timbers reminded him of a gigantic ribcage. Even in the middle of summer, the fire was blazing away in the pit, the smoke scented with herbs and crystallized tree sap. The whole house smelled expensive. The guests were dressed up in pressed linens lined with furs, in the brightest colours Far had ever seen. No one in Sheepdip would've been able to afford so luminous a blue, so vivid a red, so deep a black.

It felt like a world apart, a world he'd never even thought about before. The rest of the company fit in better, and when the Queen made his first appearance, a weird noise ran through the audience sitting on their cushioned seats, almost like a moan.

The eyes of the bride widened. Malis had been right. Saran looked radiant, the last traces of the bruises covered up and his fiery tresses gathered in a net studded with artificial pearls; he glimmered like a creature fallen from one of the stars in the summer skies. A cold little smile carved lines around his painted mouth.

For "The Green Knight," Far wore the Page's uniform again and a rather unflattering cap. There was no way he could compete in his current incarnation. He squared his shoulders and smiled back.

10
PREPARED To BiTE

WHATEVER YOU'RE DOING, PLEASE stop." Rav was pale under his makeup. "He's starting to take it seriously, and when we're preparing for our run in Seagard, I need him at the top of his game."

Far bristled at the accusation. "He was at the top of his game. Even the groom fell head over heels in love with him tonight."

Rav grimaced. "I know Per will take care of you if you want him to, but Per is no match for him. Those two have their own history."

"Saran said you persuaded him to abandon his old company."

"That's the truth. Sort of."

"Sort of?" Far wore the dress of the Evil Princess. "Can you help me with these stays? I only have a few moments before they need me on stage."

The Knight tightened and knotted the spiral-laced linen ribbons. It was clearly not the first time he'd lent a hand. They used the Hall's side chamber for the costume changes. The Princess stuck his head in to give Far the sign that they'd arranged in rehearsals, and with a last check of the wig, the Knight pushed Far back into the hall.

It was the very first time Far had played the Princess, or at least an approximation of a princess, on his way to find the path he had never seen so clearly before. It was the exciting bit of "Two Princesses, Swapped" with the audience at the edge of their seats, although they'd known all their lives how the story was to end: the evil sister would be captured and would burn in the silken flames stitched onto the cape the Sorcerer had worn the first time Far had played with the company back in Halfway.

As the evil twin he pulled the cloth over his head and swirled around until he collapsed on the flagstones of the Hall. His death was applauded, though the Princess had done all the work, had played both sisters in different shawls, something that was quick to change.

Now the virtuous sister sank weeping to the floor, helped up quickly by the Prince, who kissed and married her to bring everything to a satisfactory end, while Far knelt under the cape and tried to breathe as quietly as possible, waiting for the releasing tune that meant the end of the scene and the beginning of the epilogue.

When the melody started and the last words were spoken, the wedding guests cheered, and Far came to his feet and moved to the side. The main characters took their bows while he stepped into the changing room. He loosened the ribbons to release the stays, wiggling out of the dress that he might get to wear another time.

He looked up and saw the Queen standing in the door. Saran suddenly was very close. His scent enveloped Far and then the hands of the Queen were around his face.

"You really have an awful lot to learn." Saran leant towards him, just for a moment, but Far's knees buckled. He pushed his left hand against the wall to keep himself upright.

"Good show," Saran said. "Have you learnt all your lines for the Fairy from the Hill? They're bound to like that as well; you had them wrapped around your little finger today."

Jom came into the room. "Get a move on. They want us out of here before they start dinner."

Saran took a step back. Far began to put the costumes away, then helped Jom bring the chests into the yard, still in the underskirts that went with the dress.

"I hope I haven't interrupted anything important?" Jom asked when they pushed the last chest next to the wall outside.

Far flicked sweat from his brow. "Very fitting for the Prince to save me."

"Try not to be mean." Jom sighed. "He was really good today; I hope he can keep it up tomorrow."

"I'm not the one who started it!" Far cried in weak protest and against his better judgement.

"Yes, you are. Come on, Rav wants to have another run-through. I've never seen him so nervous about a new play."

They practised under the tarpaulin with rain dripping down around them.

As the Servant to the Fairy from the Hill, Far had a lot to say, the dialogue bouncing back and forth. Both he and Saran were starting to enjoy themselves. It was unusual that the character played by the Queen had opportunities like this; Far wondered whether Rav had kept a closer eye on them than he'd realized. He could make some of the Servant's retorts sound *very* suggestive if he allowed himself to.

Far knew why Rav had written it that way. These exchanges would make the audience like them both. They had the potential to be funny, and it would twist the knife at the end even harder. All his scenes fed off the energy around him and the Queen; it felt right to inhabit the role, like a pair of boots one had worn for a long time, perfectly formed around all the bumps.

When the Servant walked off stage, the rest of the company stood dazed for a few moments. There was a pause in the proceeding before the Young King remembered his prompt and started the next scene.

Far had never seen a play like it. He knew Rav was taking a risk. It was so unusual, the guests might take offense. They expected something they already knew, something unsurprising, and usually fairy tales were above suspicion. Every player knew they could be out on their arses in a few hours, perhaps not getting paid for the performances they'd already delivered. It was an uneasy night for all of them. Far stared at the wet wagon cover for a long time, wishing he'd had the foresight to pull Per into the hayloft before his thoughts ran wild.

He wasn't the only one worrying. The Knight turned on his mattress and Rav was the first one out at dawn, something that didn't happen too often. Far followed him into the rain-soaked grass. They had banked the fire in the evening and it only took a few slivers of wood to coax it back to life.

In the grey morning light, the Knight appeared stressed, his hair dishevelled. He knelt next to the ring of blackened stones and breathed slowly into the embers that had kept their heat during the night. Ash whirled into his face. His eyelids fluttered, the red glowing against the stubble on his cheeks.

Far stood next to him. "Should we pack up the wagons, just in case?"

"Thank you for believing so much in all of us." A tired smile slid onto Rav's face. Then he saw that Far was serious and stretched out his ink-stained hand, touching Far's forearm. "This is not the first time we've played with fire; you'll get used to the tension. You might not want to hear it, but trust him. I know, usually that's not the best of advice."

"I wouldn't trust him as far as I could throw him," Far mumbled.

The Knight chuckled; it was a deep, comforting noise. "If they don't like it, we'll switch the plays. The one with the Witches always goes down well."

"I can't help but feel responsible."

"I know, Far. I know. You could tell me a few other stories, and we could pick a new one. You always wanted your own version of "The Queen under the Lake." We could change the old one around until he agrees to play her again."

Far's bottom lip twitched, a sure sign that tears would follow. "He'd never play her for me."

"Yes, he would. He only needs an incentive. He knows there's something between you both; it's not just him feeling old and threatened by anyone who so much as glances at the corsets. If he offers to teach you, please think about it before you refuse."

Far's jaw dropped. "Teach me?"

"The Queen doesn't usually have the most lines, but as soon as she steps onto the stage, she needs to establish herself as the moral centre of the performance. It's not only how she moves, it's how she chooses to use her words. The Queen has a unique rhythm to her, and he's been the Queen for a very long time. He longs to pass on the spell, even if he's not fully aware of it yet. You could be a good Queen someday, Far. You could be the Queen under the Lake."

And as quickly as that, Far found his destiny.

It stopped raining some hours later and the rising sun dried off the yard.

At midday, Rav and the Wise King decided to risk it; they would perform outdoors, between the torches, in front of the stables. Malis helped them with the costumes. It was the first time that Far saw her pin up her husband's hair; her hands shook ever so slightly. She pulled a small basket onto her lap filled with flowers she'd gathered from the meadows around the house. She threaded them into his hair: daisies, buttercups, white and red campions; she'd even found some wild chicory. The large blue flowers stuck to him like petals punched out of the sky.

Saran noticed him lurking next to the wagon and pulled the soft shawl back over his shoulders, as if Far's gaze made him shudder.

Far, already in the long linen tunic the Servant would wear, drew closer. He'd never seen the Queen so vulnerable, his head bent to allow Malis to unwind the long strands from the knotted rags he'd slept in. For the first time, he would be Far's Fairy from the Hill.

They'd played for weeks and tried various strategies in their elaborate dance. Just the day before, Far had found himself pushed into a corner and been more than prepared to bite back, but now he sank to his knees.

He took Saran's hands and kissed both pale palms. Before it might've felt silly and even a tiny bit cruel, but on this day, he knew he'd be understood, that everything was about to change. He looked up. Saran's light brown eyes grew wide.

Far's voice cracked as he finally said it. "My Queen."

Saran bent over him and pressed a kiss to his hair, as light as a butterfly. "Will you promise to listen to me as I teach you, Far?"

Far swallowed his tears. Once again, his future turned on a heel, pushing him into a place he'd only dreamt about. "I promise," he half choked. *Maybe one day I can be him.*

Saran's voice lowered to a whisper. "Then I promise you this in turn: to protect you as my student and as a friend."

As soon as he lifted his head, Malis swooped in to kiss Far in turn. "I know we can make it work."

"Are you really sure about it, boy?" Rav was clearly exhausted, with deep dark smudges underneath his eyes, his slate-grey hair standing up in greasy strands. "It won't be an easy path for you."

The others began to gather around him, Jom and Per at the front, both wearing worried frowns. The men encircled him, each and every one a valuable piece of the company, all steering him against the side of the wagon.

How could he explain that he'd spent many hours debating with himself? That he expected Saran to fall foul as soon as they started their lessons, to be too impatient to hold back his frustrations? "I'm sure," Far said. "If I want to play the Queen one day, I need to learn from the Queen."

"On your head be it," Rav muttered, prepared to turn away.

Per caught his elbow. "No," scolded the man who played the lute. "That's not how we do things around here."

A tiny glow ignited in Far's chest.

Rav gave Far a tortured look. "Fine. If he pushes you too hard, you'll let me know, won't you?"

Far breathed deeply in relief. "I will. I promise."

"We have months of hard work ahead of us. Folk of quality are discerning wherever we play." Rav sighed. "It *would* be good to have an understudy. If things get rough again."

Per smiled at him. "There you go. I knew you had it in you."

They left the family's house in the morning. Dew sat in the cobwebs draped across the stalks in the meadow and many of the flowers hadn't opened for the day. The horses were eager to move on now that the rain had stopped, their muscles rippling under their glossy summer coats.

Far sat next to Rav on the driver's bench, his feet crossed at the ankles. They were the first wagon on the road winding back into the western forest. The harnesses jangled, and the wheels had a slight squeak to them, despite Far going around with a pot of lard an hour ago, smearing it deep into the places where wood rubbed against wood.

In the back, Saran slept, buried under a heap of quilted blankets. From time to time a soft snore made its way out of his cocoon, while Malis's voice drifted over from one of the wagons behind them. She sang a song Far knew from his village, a simple melody with words coloured by joy.

We have many more weddings to play at, Far thought, *and many more roads to travel to reach them. One day, I will look back on today and believe I was as happy as I could ever be, with leaves painting their shadows on the top of my head and rehearsals scheduled for the midday break. One day, I will have learnt all I can from the man I almost fell in love with.*

PART II

TJOR & SEAGARD

1
AGAINST ALL EVENTUALITIES

T JOR NA TIALIN WAS late, maybe too late to be
let in. He would miss it, and he'd looked forward
to the day for weeks. Taking the afternoon off always
involved an inexplicable amount of paperwork, all
for a few hours away from the dusty ledgers and
ink-stained desks. It had been difficult to secure the
tickets; the whole city seemed set on seeing this
particular play and he had to pay more for them than
expected. He'd had to use some of his savings. He
couldn't risk missing it.

Why, oh why did all these people have to leave
their houses at this exact time to block his way? There
were a couple of baker's carts and a large group of
apprentices in their black robes, members of the

Company of the Bull by the looks of it, already half drunk and ready to pick a fight with anyone who tried to push past them. Especially him.

"Oi, watch it, stupid!"

Tjor was used to it. As soon as three or more of them gathered, it always required effort to extract himself. He hated them, had hated them since starting his job on the harbour bridge. Wearing his work clothes made it worse; he was easily identifiable, and if he ever had any idea of pushing back, of not lowering his gaze and rushing on, someone would surely report him.

To think that he'd been so excited when the letter came to accept him. His sister had laughed and kissed him in delight, and even his father had seemed a bit happier, at least for a few days. Tjor's salary helped the family, or what coin was left of it after he paid for room and board.

It had been strange to move out and find himself a good day's walk away in a world that was decidedly different from what he was used to. He'd been to Seagard many times but had never attempted a life there before. Its wide roads and colourful merchant houses suddenly became less welcoming, more menacing. Someone of his background would never have been accepted as a student. He'd only been given a few days of training, then sent to the administration and records office of the Company, a junior clerk at the very end of the food chain who still got finger cramps and by now had lost all illusions.

Seagard was one of the largest cities on the Continent, famous for its hustle and bustle, the port from which whole fleets left for the Spice Isles. Tjor had hoped to be part of the glory and found himself shoved to the back. The Honourable Company of the Gull needed people like him, but they avoided admitting as much.

He'd done better than his father—much better than his grandfather, who had worked on the docks until he'd been crushed to pulp under a consignment of sugar loaves. The compensation had bought something like an education for his eldest son, Tjor's father, who had hatched the plan to send his own son to town.

In a few years, Tjor would be in a good position to marry and pass the torch on to the next generation, a son who would also sit for hours and hours in the dark rooms at the back of the house, endlessly copying out correspondence—not the interesting bits, but the everyday communications that were just important enough to be preserved in the records.

Every Company on the Blue Bridge had their version of his office, but the rivalries between them made it difficult for their staff to compare notes. There were three other clerks he had to work with, but no one as low of rank. Tjor was responsible for everything no one else wanted to do, especially dealing with the minutes that were sent down from above. The First Gull had the worst handwriting Tjor had ever seen, and his official secretary wasn't much better; he also employed his own set of abbreviations and sometimes they took hours to decipher.

Tjor had to write out three copies of everything; the head clerk was partial to multiple backups. One set was kept in the house, the others sent to undisclosed locations. A few centuries ago, all the houses on the Blue Bridge had burned down, and the Companies were determined to prepare against all eventualities. Not that anyone would've been interested to read the grievances aired in the last meetings with the station masters of the eastern posts. They mainly involved pickled herrings.

Nevertheless, he'd spent all morning on the papers, and when the bell finally rang to signal his release, he'd tried to get out of the office as quickly as possible. He was still late, because the senior clerk had given him one last errand. He was ordered to collect a parcel of proofs from the printers in Owlgate in the eastern part of town, but the theatre lay to the west. He had lost his way twice trying to cross the main road that split Seagard into two distinctive halves.

As a minor employee of the Company, he was not supposed to visit the Westown quarters, but he'd seen the posters everywhere. Before moving to Seagard, he'd imagined himself at the theatres all the time, as the admission prices were not that expensive if he was prepared to stand for a few hours. Then he'd realized his working hours covered all of the afternoon performances, and in the evenings he found it difficult to motivate himself.

Today was different. Today should've been well-organized and the best gift he'd ever given his sister.

She was waiting for him in Crooked Lane and must by now be very worried. Ever since she had planned to visit their cousins for a few days this winter, she had looked forward to seeing him in his new element. Now he would arrive covered in sweat, lugging the heavy proofs with him, his boots splattered with mud. He had promised to meet her in good time; Westown was not a suitable place for a young woman to wait all on her own, though his sister generally had her wits about her and was not above fashioning one of her hatpins into a weapon. Hopefully she had asked their cousin to accompany her.

When he had started his lessons, years ago, they'd planned her visit, and he was about to spoil their dream because he'd been afraid to deny his colleague's request—and because he hadn't dared to ignore the mission altogether and find an excuse to do it the next day. He'd been trained to be useful, helpful, and friendly; it probably would be his downfall one day.

He reached Westown. He was not supposed to know about the shortcuts, but he knew them anyway and stepped into the filthy narrow side streets, the timber frame façades leaning uncomfortably close to his head. Most of the windows were covered in paper and wooden slats. Every building showed signs of shoddy repair work, desperate attempts to keep the structures as close to habitable as possible. The smell that rose from the dwellings was familiar: cabbage and clothes that had not been washed in a long time. Westown was where his family had originated and what his mother was trying to keep them away from.

It was why they'd left the city and paid for his lessons, so he could help keep his sister safe.

He noticed the noises coming from his mouth, long rasping gulps, and still he ran through the labyrinth of rubbish heaps that built up as soon as the weather turned cold, when people stopped spending much time outside and simply pushed what they wanted to get rid of out the door.

He reached the Crooked Gate desperately out of breath, almost fell onto the wider street in front of him, and stopped short. A lot of people were milling around the entrance to the playhouse.

He instantly spotted his sister, her black hair topped with a broad-brimmed fur hat that had a couple of particularly long pins sticking out of it, their blunt ends topped with green glass beads. She wore her best shawl, dyed a rusty red, and her dress was quite new, cut to simulate the recent fashions and of a deep pine green that he always loved to see on her. "Tjor—Heavens, breathe!"

"How long ... how long have you waited?"

"I only just arrived. What—oh, you miscounted the bells again, didn't you? It's really quite early. I didn't expect you to be here yet. You look horrible. Here, I managed to sneak out something." She pulled a small leather flask from her shoulder bag. When she pulled out the cork, Tjor's eyes watered.

"Thank you, but ...." He finally managed to draw breath. She was right; he must've miscounted. It happened often, but it had been a good while since he'd gone into such a panic about it. He would've been able to take the long way around, to arrive at the theatre with a healthy glow and eyes brightened by the exercise instead of in a big sweaty mess.

She gave him a folded-up handkerchief, which instantly went limp and soggy when he pressed it to his burning face.

"They haven't even opened the gates yet. You have plenty of time to calm down. How was your day?"

He stared at her, and she started to laugh. "While you're busy wiping yourself down, *my* day was already quite eventful." She adjusted the knitted shawl knotted around her shoulders. "One proposal out of the way."

Tjor blinked. "Did you let him down gently?"

"He knows it can't go anywhere. I remember him chewing on his teething ring. I had planned to take him with me today, but after that particular demonstration of exceedingly poor judgement, I decided to risk coming on my own."

"He wouldn't have been able to get a ticket anyway. It's been sold out for days."

She shrugged. "I dare say he wouldn't have minded too much. At least now I'm free to have a look around without him breathing down my neck on Mother's orders."

"I'm sure she was joking."

"She wasn't. She expects me to make good use of my time here. She wouldn't approve of you taking me to Crooked Lane. It's not what she had in mind for us."

"The play's only on here. It might move to one of the bigger houses later but at least we can say we saw it in Crooked Lane before everyone had the chance."

"Well, that already sounds more like Mother. I'm sure I can sell it to her somehow. Maybe I'll just lie."

He sighed unhappily. "You shouldn't do that, Tjovis."

"She started it. She said this hat makes me look like a bear." Tjovis glowered defiantly at him.

"Well ...."

She grinned. "I like bears. Feeling better?"

Tjor had certainly cooled down. He shivered. "Yes."

"I hope you haven't forgotten to bring the tickets. Would be a shame if you had to run all the way back to the Blue Bridge."

"I've got the tickets."

"Have you checked?"

She knew him altogether too well. "A few times."

She drew a deep breath. "I'll buy us a bag of hazelnuts to go with the apple brandy. Watching a sensational new play always makes me hungry."

2
A SINGLE BREATH

H**E'D BOUGHT MORE EXPENSIVE** seats than he usually would, so they could sit in the gallery and catch up properly.

The playhouse in Crooked Lane was one of the oldest in Seagard but quite small. During the winter months, touring companies came for a fixed number of performances, trying out new material. From time to time, something took off unexpectedly and everyone flocked to the theatre to be part of it. Already, four new plays featured waterhorses—none as good as the original, but other companies had identified an opportunity, and everyone was already speculating what monster could be next.

Barely anyone had heard of waterhorses before the craze started. The play was supposed to be very loosely based on an obscure legend from the Hillakes district, far beyond the southern hills, almost where the northern woods began, somewhere exciting but still relatable. Everyone had learnt that waterhorses were wicked and weirdly attractive, and that combination was the best to get people talking. It had brought Tjor and Tjovis to Westown along with many other spectators clearly used to the clean avenues of Eastown. The galleries were bursting with well-dressed people.

Tjor saw the group of apprentices he'd met on his way had found a place in front of the stage, sharing a skin of wine. Quite a few Company members milled around, most of them apprentices in black robes with coloured braids, but he also spotted a few students, sticking out of the crowd like fruit jellies. The Suns wore yellow, the Bulls red, the Unicorns blue, and the Gulls, Tjor's own employers, had chosen an unfortunate white that always looked grubby and was often replaced by grey for practical reasons. He spotted three Unicorns and a few Suns, all in the pit.

"What's wrong?" Tjovis flicked a few nutshells from her dress.

"Keeping an eye on the wolves."

Suddenly she looked concerned, her green eyes narrowed. "You don't mean that."

"They are literally everywhere. At least they're easy to spot. I wish they wouldn't make me wear my own colours though. They all like to kick downwards. And this doesn't make it easier."

"What?"

"This." He gestured at himself. He'd always been tall and rather fat and for some reason the combination did something to the young men around him. He looked like something they should try to dominate, standing at least half a head above them all. At the same time, his apparent softness led them to believe it would be easier than expected.

Before becoming a clerk for the Gulls, he'd at least theoretically been able to push back. Now he was part of the hierarchy of the Companies. He did not have their training. Even students in their first year were better schooled than him and had passed a series of tests in order to wear their colours. He just happened to be able to write, and though he was able to hold a full lecture on the pickled herring trade in the eastern lands, they would always know exactly where he stood, even if he sat in the galleries for one precious day. At least he didn't have to pretend with Tjovis. She knew about him.

She didn't look at him when she said, "Seen anyone interesting? They can't all be horrible."

"But they are, the whole lot."

"Even the pretty ones?"

"Especially the pretty ones."

"Shame. Mother would squeal in delight if I announced my engagement to one of them. Imagine, marrying into one of the Founding Families."

"I don't know whether I'd be able to breathe."

"Breathing is very overrated. Breeding, on the other hand …."

He felt himself go red. "Maybe one of the Unicorns? The one in the middle?"

"The one with the dark blond curls? Blue really *is* his colour, wouldn't you say?"

"He certainly wears it well."

She snorted, then lightly touched his elbow. "I've missed this. If I'd accepted his proposal today, I would have lived here. We could've met up every week, seen lots of other plays, gone out for chocolate …."

"The tickets almost ruined me. I won't be able to afford chocolate for a long time."

"I have half a silverling to spend on a new hat. I'll take you out afterwards to make up for the tickets."

"You really don't need to."

"I want to. Surely you can't refuse such a measly request when your sister came all this way just to visit you?"

"All this way?" he asked quietly.

"The roads were very muddy."

"At least you got a proposal out of it. Maybe two, if you manage to separate this particular Unicorn from the herd." He had missed their conversations as well. Their whole life people had remarked on how similar the siblings were and had treated them more like twins. He rarely felt like the older brother.

She smirked. "All the students come from money, don't they?"

"At least they pretend they do. He might be lovely to look at, but chances are his father lives on credit,

Founding Family or no. Many of the Gulls do—and they forget the clerks copy out the warning letters for the archives."

People were still streaming into the pit. The level of noise in the house rose from moment to moment and they were unlikely to be overheard. Tjor tried to relax but a muscle between his shoulders kept bunching up, the result of working squashed into his desk for months.

No one was here to look at him. They had all come for the players. Some of them might wonder if he was allowed in the galleries but might assume his sister had paid for him to be here. Her hat was certainly big and furry enough to suggest the possibility, and she wore it with a confidence that utterly eluded him. No wonder their cousin had felt compelled to propose.

The group of Unicorns had been pushed uncomfortably close to the Suns and a few rude gestures were being exchanged. Other members of the expectant audience positioned themselves between the students, clearly aware of the implications. No one wanted to risk the play not being performed because students got into a fist fight. Tjor noticed the Unicorn with the dark blond curls had moved to the outer edge of his group, avoiding contact with the Suns. Perhaps he was a coward—or merely a bit cleverer than the others.

A drum started and a hush fell over the pit. Everyone turned around. A flute joined in. Tjor held his breath. It was the first time he felt part of the people of Seagard, not just the low-ranking newcomer who had to hide his ambitions. He hadn't seen a play in ages and shuddered in anticipation. In a few moments, he would know what the whole town was talking about; he would see the Waterhorse, the famous costume with the mane made from green silk. He would hear the deep seductive voice of the monster.

Two players stepped onto the stage and the crowd muttered in irritation. He had never seen a play where the characters weren't introduced before the start, a long row of dressed-up men. The play began without warning, with a scene in the Castle, the Prince disobeying his father using words Tjor had always wanted to say but never been able to.

The Prince felt badly treated; he never wanted to marry, nor be sold off to the Fairies. No self-respecting father should ever have made such a stupid deal, especially not standing over the infant's cradle, on a deep winter's night, during a snowstorm. No wonder the Fairies had taken it seriously.

The Prince would leave the Castle, find his own way and lots of fascinating new friends while he was at it, maybe even a wandering bard with a magical lute. The possibilities were endless. It was summer and the Hillakes covered in blossom. Somewhere there was sure to be a Princess he could fall in love with at first sight—that was what always happened, so he was fully entitled to expect it.

The Prince, dark-skinned and with the widest smile Tjor had ever seen, reminded him of the Gulls' apprentices. Surely the Prince was not supposed to make him feel like that? The Prince saved the Princess, and then they were married because that was how it *worked*. But Tjor was relieved to see him leave the stage.

A gauzy cloth unfurled at the back, covered with tree roots cut from rough linen, and a velvet-covered bench was pushed out of the wings. The audience was no longer in the Castle; they were under the Hills. A hooded figure scurried onto the stage.

The scene started when the Fairy shrugged off her cloak and the audience gasped appreciatively. The boy who played the Fairy from the Hill was lanky and pale, his eyes wide and dark. His hair had obviously been dyed for the part, the same colour as Tjovis's shawl, and was studded with blue flowers made from silk. It did not look like a wig and fell almost to his belt.

Tjor's own nails dug into his knees.

The Fairy smiled up to the galleries with a confidence that made Tjor break out in sweat again. He felt the gaze travelling over his face. It seemed to linger on him, just for a breath. A Servant in a long tunic entered, and together they mirrored the dialogue that happened before in the Castle. The Fairy really could not be expected to go ahead with it. She was too old for him; maybe if she had been blessed with a daughter, but the Prince would never honour or begin to understand the ways of the Folk of the Hill. Her Servant agreed with his face unmoved, but with words meant to be misinterpreted. The audience soon erupted into chuckles whenever he spoke, applauding when the Fairy caught on to his game.

The Fairy was much too clever for the arrogant Prince. Her eyes sparkled, and she laughed, her red hair shaking with it, the flowers bright blue stars. Tjor had long since stopped waiting for the Waterhorse.

3
SOMETHING EXTRAORDINARY

T JOR HAD FALLEN IN love a few times in his life, usually with boys who looked as if he'd made them up, all blond locks and dimpled smiles, but growing up a mere day's walk from Seagard, he had always known to keep such feelings to himself. His sister had known, of course, because he needed someone to talk to, because she was able to see right through him anyway. There was no point in pretending.

Only two weeks after he'd moved to the city, he'd noticed the posters advertising the next round of executions. On the list glued to the outside of the house he slept in were men to be hanged for "unnatural conduct." He stayed far away from

Temple Market that day, but registered the excited hum that swept through Eastown. Like upstanding citizens everywhere, the people of Seagard loved their public executions.

He had felt more desperate than usual for a few weeks after but tried to bury himself in work, a strategy that made him fall even harder when the Fairy from the Hill looked directly at him, at no one else for that entire moment.

It was the first time in his life he was without doubt.

He had always found it rather unfair that the Princes in plays were allowed to kiss men on stage, that it was even *expected* of them. On that square of wooden boards above the pit and below the galleries, the laws of the Continent followed a different path, but even if his father had considered giving permission for his son to pursue that type of career, Tjor knew all too well that no one would've thought him Prince material.

There were strictly no Princesses in his future, and he had made his peace with it; the world needed more junior clerks than Princes anyway. At some point his parents would suggest someone for him to marry, and he would accept the new chore as he had all the others. After all, he had been trained well. But on that one afternoon at the Crooked Lane playhouse, everything he thought he knew about his life turned inside out, like a hastily removed sock.

He felt nauseated, light-headed, and his eyes watered because he couldn't bear to blink as long as the Fairy was on stage. Afterwards, he couldn't remember much of the play at all, even though Tjovis raved about the Waterhorse; Tjor only recalled that the true villain of the piece had been played by another man with red hair, which might have been a deliberate choice or just a coincidence. Based on his sister's reaction, he must've been good, but Tjor had barely noticed the famous horse-head contraption.

He existed in his own bubble of fear and longing, and when the Fairy was unmasked at the end and it transpired that there had been two characters in the story classed as villains—even though for two hours a whole house filled with people had passionately rooted for them—his heart seemed to stop, just stop. There was no way he could afford to see the play again, and he would not be allowed another afternoon off before the holidays. The players belonged to a travelling company; they wouldn't stay in town much longer. He would lose whatever he'd found the moment he left his seat. He was not able to applaud when the players took their bows at the end; he tried to cross his arms, hold himself steady, will himself back into the life he led in the city.

He flinched when Tjovis jumped up. "That was amazing. I'm so glad you suggested it. I'm ready for a bowl of chocolate, come on." She pushed against him. Perhaps for the first time in their lives she didn't realize how much he was struggling to keep it together.

All the other people had left the galleries. They were the last ones, and it took him two tries to get up. He followed his sister onto the creaky stairs and out into the road, where he finally managed to turn around.

One of the pasted-on flyers had partly come loose from the advertising post. He tried to peel it off, but wasn't able to get all of it, only the top bit. At least he had the name of the play and the company. He pushed the scrap of sticky paper into the inner pocket of his coat, shouldered the bag with the proofs, and closed his eyes. He was so used to letting go; it should not have been a problem.

Tjovis took his elbow. "Do you know of a good place? I'm going to throw in a plate of lemon squares ...." She stopped. "Tjor? What's wrong?"

He bit his lip until it hurt. "Everything."

Tjovis had chosen the chocolate house because it was freshly painted and close to the main road, which also meant it was more expensive than the establishments Tjor was used to. *The Elegant Macaroon* catered to women being taken out by their husbands, brothers, or fathers for a treat. It was clean and had upholstered chairs. Each table was decorated with a sprig of ivy, and it smelled of boiled chocolate and freshly baked cakes.

Tjovis ordered the signature macaroons and two rounds of chocolate, then carefully removed the three pins from her hat. "Tell me," she said.

"There's nothing to tell," he muttered.

"A lot happened. We just saw a really good play and I intend to yell at everyone about it. And now we are having outrageously expensive biscuits."

"Apart from that."

She frowned. "I don't understand."

"I'm not sure that I understand it myself." He shuddered. "Do you think it's possible to fall in love at first sight?" *It's a nice idea in the tales, but it feels very scary.*

She blinked a few times. "They were characters in a play," she said quietly.

"I'm not talking about the characters."

"You couldn't see his face for most of the play; he had the thing on!"

"It's not the man who played the Waterhorse. It's the one who looked at me."

"You can't fall in love with the Fairy from the Hill." She sounded serious, very worried, as if he'd confessed to loving an actual fairy from the mound.

"Why not?" he whispered.

"Nothing that he was on the stage was real. He wore a bucket of face paint and probably a wig."

"I'm not concerned with the costume, Tjovis. When he looked at me, he *looked* at me. I'm sure of it." Tears rose in his eyes, tears he couldn't afford to shed.

She sighed and took his hand in hers. "I know you're lonely, but this sounds ...."

"Stupid?" he whispered.

"'Deranged' was the word I was looking for. There are places they put people who have these kinds of thoughts. You need to be careful, Tjor. Please."

He dashed the back of his hand against his flaming cheek. "Trust me, I know. It just feels weird."

"Weird in what way?"

"As if the whole world has shifted. I never knew this was possible. For me, I mean."

She stared at him in dismay. "Why shouldn't it be possible for you?"

"You know ... because I'm different."

The boy serving their food and drinks appeared next to the table and they waited with bated breath until he finally put down the last bowl and left. When Tjor looked up again, his sister's eyes were suspiciously shiny. "You're not that different."

"Everyone treats me as if I am. I always thought it was a bad thing, until he looked at me today." Tjor pulled the flat porcelain bowl, in which chocolate was traditionally served in Seagard, towards himself, and took a tiny sip. Every house had its customized recipe, and the *Macaroon*'s patrons obviously liked it very sweet.

Tjovis chose one of the crispy milknut biscuits and took a big bite, something their mother would have scolded her for at home, but they were not at home. They were on their own, and the world still had not gone back to normal.

"Try one. They're nice." She sniffled quietly. "What are you going to do?"

He put down the delicate bowl and shrugged. "What can I do?"

"Don't you want to go back?"

"Of course I do. At the very least to find out if that was really what he meant or if it's just in my head. He might only have noticed me because I stuck out so much. Next to all the well-dressed men in the galleries, no one expects a clerk in a shabby uniform."

"What if you're right? What if it was ... something extraordinary? Why shouldn't it happen to you?" she repeated.

"I'm not allowed to expect it. At least, that's how it's always felt. Even talking about it sounds ridiculous. So what if he was interested? What would that mean?"

"Maybe you're going to live happily ever after." Tjovis ate a second macaroon, and Tjor quickly secured one of the biscuits for himself, setting it carefully down next to his half-drunk chocolate.

"There's no such thing. For anyone."

She smiled at him. "Perhaps you're right. You could at least talk to him, find out his name."

I might be wrong. Fearfully, catastrophically wrong. "Maybe tomorrow."

"Tjor, if you don't go back today you won't ever go. Don't worry about me. I'll find my way back to Aunt Alis's. I still have a few days left, and we can meet up when you've finished work tomorrow. I'm sure I can persuade him to walk me down to the harbour, even in the dark, and then you can tell me everything."

"That's not going to work, and you know it." *If I'm wrong, I might not survive the night.*

"Can't you come up to the house for dinner?"

"Aunt Alis hasn't invited me yet."

"I'll ask them. Please!"

"You're getting too invested in this, Tjovis. It's not going to work." The realization settled heavy on his chest.

Suddenly she sat up very straight. "Tjor—look, but don't look."

His eyes closed in exasperation. "What?"

She made a weird grimace, as if she was trying to point something out using only her eyebrows. "Is that him?"

He turned on his chair and glanced over his shoulder.

In the middle of the *Elegant Macaroon* stood someone in a rumpled linen shirt, with only the left trouser leg stuffed into his boot, his face pale and smudged around the eyes. Eyes unmistakably the eyes of the Fairy from the Hill.

4
INTREPID

THE BOY PULLED TJOR out into the street, and after noticing some of the *Macaroon*'s guests staring at them through the windows, around the corner to the gate that led onto Plum Lane. "I know how it sounds ...." he began.

Standing so close to him, Tjor saw freckles through the remnants of the greasepaint. He only had to bend his neck a bit to look at him; the boy was taller than expected.

"No, I was just debating going back to ... to find you. My name is Tjor, by the way."

"Far. Faral actually, but no one bothers with the long version. Was this your first time in Crooked Lane?"

Tjor managed a slow nod. "I've been in Seagard for a while but not seen any plays."

"We're only here for a while." The boy who played the Fairy looked at his boots and scratched his head helplessly, dislodging a blue flower that had hidden itself away. It fell between them.

Tjor bent down to pick it up. The silk felt warm between his shaking fingers.

Far stared at his hand, glanced up, and something changed in his face. He stepped closer and touched Tjor, just for a moment. "We need to meet somewhere else. We're lodging at *The Broken Ladle*, just off Crooked Lane. You work on the Bridge?"

Tjor nodded again. "Living in White Bear Yard, but it's Company accommodation."

Far gave him a tight smile. "Then it has to be the *Ladle*. I can let them know, if you want to."

Tjor barely managed to swallow as excitement fluttered up his throat. "Yes, of course I want to." His own voice sounded strange; it had gone a bit squeaky.

Far let out a deep, shuddering breath. "I'm not going mad, am I? Sometimes it's difficult to tell what's real and what's the stage."

Tjor chewed his lower lip. "We might both be going mad then. Can two people go mad at the same time?" He studied the smudged face of the boy in front of him. "Does it happen in any of the stories?"

Far laughed suddenly. It was different than the laugh he'd used for the Fairy, more of a giggle. "Not that I can recall. Come tomorrow. It's rehearsal day and I'm free in the evening ... Tjor. Have I remembered that correctly? Good, I need to go."

Tjor loosened a shaky laugh. "I need to return to my sister."

Far backed out of the Plumgate. "See you tomorrow. Please don't forget. You can keep the flower; I'll make another one."

When Tjor sat down again, all eyes in the room were glued to him. In his absence, the second round of chocolate had arrived. Tjovis had finished his first bowl while she waited. "I've bitten all my nails to the quick," she hissed. "What happened? What did he want?"

"He invited me to see the players."

"In the theatre?"

"No, not in the theatre as such." He finished his second chocolate in one gulp. "We shouldn't stay here. Have you paid?"

She shook her head.

"I'll take care of that. Get your things together. I'll walk you to Aunt Alis's and we'll talk on the way."

In a few hours, the city had changed for him. He felt dazed, and it was difficult to walk in a straight line. When they reached the main road, his sister took his elbow, pressed it against her side. It took them a while to reach the crossing into the Printer's Quarter.

"You said, we'd talk, so talk."

None of it feels real. "What do you want me to say? I'm going to see him tomorrow."

"But you know that you haven't imagined it. He came for you, for Heaven's sake!"

"Ouch. You're squeezing so hard you're going to leave a bruise!"

She dug her nails into his arm. "Because it's exciting!"

"You can't tell anyone about it, especially not Aunt Alis."

"I won't, I promise."

"Tjovis, this is serious." He thought about the execution posters in White Bear Yard, then shook his head. Nothing had happened yet, nothing at all. Maybe nothing would continue to happen, even at *The Broken Ladle*. He always expected the worst outcomes, and simply because Far had touched his temple, just above the ear, it did not mean that Tjor would be allowed to kiss him. *But maybe I'm wrong again. Maybe I'm putting my head into the noose as we speak.*

They stepped through Owlgate and the strap of Tjor's bag bit into his shoulder. He had carried the proofs all over town to arrive back on the doorstep of the printer's shop. He could've waited and collected them later, but he had been so eager to prove his worth. Yet tomorrow evening he would bend the rules as far as he'd ever dared to.

Aunt Alis's house was situated on one of the back lanes of the quarter that had smartened up considerably over recent years. The doorstep was scoured, the windows glazed with small square panes, and the glow of the sitting room fire fell onto their faces. He'd been so wrapped up in the possibilities, he barely noticed that darkness had come over the city.

Tjovis let him go and kissed his cheek. "We're going to meet on your lunchbreak, the day after tomorrow," she commanded. "I'll come down to the harbour. Wait on the Bridge and I'll organize a day for you to come to dinner."

He nodded and watched her being let into the house. As soon as the door closed behind her, he realized he was starving. He'd only had one biscuit with his chocolate and a few hazelnuts at the theatre. But he had also paid at the *Macaroon* and had very little money left. The street vendors closed soon after dark, and there would be nothing in his rooms. He was supposed to eat in the refectory at the House of the Gulls.

On his way south, he deliberately used the smaller streets and came across a baker's cart returning from its last round. He bought two of the cheapest brown loaves and instantly tore into the first one, almost choking on the dry crust. How on Earth was he supposed to wait? He finished the first loaf when he reached the Yard and stuffed the second one into the bag with the printer's proofs. He was still hungry, but it was better to hide his food from the others.

White Bear Yard lay deep in the Harbour Quarter, one of the shabbier neighbourhoods, though considered good enough for the people working on the Bridge who were not members of the Companies. The buildings were converted storerooms. Similar complexes stood all over the quarter, often quite close together. While the students and apprentices demonstrated their rivalries, the staff were expected to hold their peace, but not mingle.

Two beds had been placed to a room, but Tjor had had his own space since he started with the Gulls. The torches in the Yard illuminated the small room. His stuff was piled on the spare bed. Apart from the beds there were two chairs and the washstand, and a wooden box that could be locked and in which he kept his books and a few of Tjovis's letters.

He sank to the floor, pulled the ripped piece of the flyer and the squashed silk flower from his jacket, and squirreled them away. He was too afraid of losing them, though he dearly wished to keep them with him always. He took off his boots and lay on the bed fully clothed. Was that not exactly what he'd wanted? Getting a job in Seagard had meant excitement, meeting new people every day, a big life—until he understood that working for one of the Companies meant life was supposed to be small and he was no more than a useful hand, writing, writing, always writing. The flickering lights on the whitewashed ceiling echoed the rapid beating of his heart, the bird trying to smash through the bars of its cage.

The Broken Ladle was one of the city's ancient institutions, connected to the theatres of Westown for a very long time. As it was not forced to attract outsiders, its general aspect was one of gentle neglect. Its beds were always booked and the furniture in the taproom polished by thousands of hands and trouser seats, some of them belonging to players who became famous later on in their careers. The building had three stories, the top floor completely given over to Far's company to afford them privacy during the strenuous weeks of their engagement. The suite included a common room with a large fireplace, accessible from the corridor outside and used for all sorts of meetings.

When Tjor was shown in, the servant did not seem to find it strange that someone would come all the way up from the Blue Bridge; they must've assumed some sort of business proposal and left him alone. Tjor considered whether he was supposed to sit down or remain standing; he searched his sleeves for lint and stray hairs. He had tried to appear well-groomed and promptly broken his comb. It was hard to achieve the desired effect with just half of it and he knew he would need to buy a new one soon, another expense he had not foreseen. He had pulled a short cloak on when leaving the office to hide his uniform, but the common room was warm, and a drop of sweat collected in his left eyebrow.

He sighed, unpinned the simple iron brooch that held the cloak in place, and draped the cloth over one of the empty chairs. Was he too early again? He had taken care to count out the peals of the bell, but maybe he had run quicker than he thought, or Far had changed his mind, decided in the morning that extending an invitation to someone he did not know was stupid. His knuckles started to hurt; he'd gripped the back of the chair too hard for quite some time.

"There you are."

A man he did not know by name entered the room through one of the doors in the back. "He was getting worried; thought you might've thought better of it." Tjor recognized him as one of the musicians, the one who played the lute. "I'll let him know you've arrived."

Did all the company members guess why he was here? He tried to swallow, but the other door opened and the man who played the Waterhorse came into the room, almost as tall as Tjor himself, his hair bound back from his face and in simple linen clothing. He was barefoot, though it was winter. "Has someone gone to tell him?"

Tjor nodded.

The Waterhorse gestured towards the table. "We'll eat soon. I hope you'll join us?"

"If Far wants me to stay?" he asked nervously.

"Oh, you're a polite one." The Waterhorse laid his head to one side and studied him. "You should know that he's well-loved and protected. Every single one of us would come after you, if ...." The man was powerfully built. Tjor wasn't often in a position to feel threatened. He tucked in his chin, drew up his shoulders on pure instinct.

"Saran, leave him alone." Far stepped between them. "You scared him. He looks as if he's about to turn around and run away." He smiled at Tjor. "Are you going to run away?"

Tjor shook his head, and both red-haired men grinned at him.

Saran sighed. "Polite and intrepid, how fun."

5
TEMPTED

TJOR WAS INTRODUCED TO the rest of the company, who clearly preferred informal clothes on their day off. He was astonished to see a woman among them, though of course she would not be permitted to perform. All of them gave him a quick check over, and he forgot their names immediately when Far ushered him to the short end of the large table.

"Sit. Would you like a drink?"

"Maybe some apple juice." It was strange. He felt as if he was being interviewed for another job.

Someone passed an earthenware jug and two mugs down to them. "Have you been in Seagard long?"

"Not quite a year."

"Do you like working for the Gulls?"

Tjor decided to be honest. "Meh. I'm sure it's the same in all the other administration offices on the Bridge."

Far seemed taken aback. "Offices?"

"I'm the junior clerk with the Gulls."

"But your hands are clean." Far pushed a filled mug over to him. "I always thought inklings had ink-stained hands."

Tjor blinked. "I wash."

Far snorted. "That's not what I meant. I thought you did other things around the house."

"No, I just ... write."

"Have you always known how?"

"Well, since I was four. My father made sure of it. He wanted me to be able to come to the city and work for the Companies."

"I'm still learning," Far said. "My reading has improved a lot, at least that's what Rav tells me, but when I write I forget the shapes sometimes and they end up the wrong way around."

"It's supposed to be more difficult if you start later in life."

Far shrugged. "At least I'm trying to keep my end of the bargain. All players need to read and write."

Tjor blinked. "I didn't know that was a requirement Kent. It must be difficult for you."

"Not many can write where I come from. Did you also grow up far away from here?"

"No. It takes a day to get home, heading east. One of those villages that form near an important road.

Originally my family is from Seagard, but we moved out there a generation ago, so it made sense for me to come back, and I still have relatives here. My sister is staying with them at the moment, and I was taking her to the theatre and of course I had heard about the play and ...."

"Breathe," Far said quietly. He stretched out his hand and his fingertips brushed Tjor's knee. Before he could think about it, he caught Far's hand and closed his own around it. The Waterhorse had called him "intrepid." Perhaps he really could be. For a moment none of them said anything, then Tjor took a deep breath. "I don't know how to do this."

"I probably do. Heavens, your eyes are really green. Don't look so shocked. You're not very good with compliments, are you?"

"I'm not used to them."

"I can tell. How old are you?"

"Nineteen summers, but my birthday isn't too far away."

"Have your parents tried to marry you off yet?"

"No specific action has been taken. They're currently concentrating on my sister. She's not my twin, only a year younger. It would be great if you could meet her. I ...." He bit his lip. "Normally I don't talk this much. Only when I'm nervous."

Far covered their joined hands with the fingers of his left. "I always talk a lot. Some people find it annoying." His glance strayed over to the others who had started to set the table with wooden platters, knives, spoons, and napkins. They tried not to disturb

Tjor and Far too much but obviously followed their conversation. They were surely used to sharing most of their lives with each other.

Tjor felt a weird pang of jealousy. They must never feel alone, travelling everywhere together and now getting famous; it was an experience they all shared. He did not belong here. He was one of the audience, a mere spectator, but Far still held on to his hands as if he wanted to pull Tjor closer but was afraid to do so under the watchful gaze of the Waterhorse.

The way in which the older red-headed man had tried to frighten him worried Tjor. Were they related? They did not look like each other, apart from the hair. Far's hair was dyed, he reminded himself. As if he had tried to resemble the other, or maybe the Fairy from the Hill just had red hair and he hated wearing the wigs.

The door opened, and Far let go as the *Ladle*'s kitchen servants brought in their meal. Tjor leaned back in his chair, trying not to look too flustered. He desperately wanted to touch Far again. Just the tips of their fingers would have been plenty, merely to know it was real.

They watched the food coming to the table: different cheeses, cold roasted meats, apple sauce, pickled vegetables, and eggs. Tjor had been living off the watery stews served in the refectory for months and could not help gawping.

"Most of our salary is paid in food and accommodation," Far explained. "It has been a very successful run. Come, let's eat. I've only had a slice of plum cake since rehearsals. Bread?" He grabbed one of the reed baskets. "Oh wait, these are the sweet ones."

"Sweet is good," Tjor said.

Far smiled. "I'm quite addicted to cinnamon. I'm from out in the sticks, not a lot of spices there."

"Out in the sticks?"

"Sheepdip-on-Lightwater in the Hillakes."

"I've heard of the Hillakes. Are they as beautiful as they say?"

"They are, but alas, no cinnamon. At first, I found the food here a bit strange, but now I'm so used to it, it'll be hard to leave."

"Where will you go next?" *How quickly will I lose you?*

"It's my first time starting off from Seagard, but I assume that we'll go towards the Northeast first, then follow the road to Eastbay, and come back down south in a circle. But on the way there might be other engagements, for which we'll need to zig-zag a bit. In the summer we played at a wedding in the Great Western Woods; that was interesting. I can't believe that was only a few months ago—so much has happened in the meantime. That was the first time we tested 'The Waterhorse'. Back then Saran played the Fairy."

Tjor swallowed a mouthful of almond cake. "Why did he stop?"

"We lost our Evil Sorcerer on the way back east. He caught the cough, and we had to leave him with his family in Smallford. We had to get a bit creative, and Saran has by far the best voice." He leaned closer. "Don't tell him, but the play would have never taken off with the old Waterhorse. Not in this way. To be honest, it's been quite a shock. The cheese is really good, if you like them runny and stinky. Jom, can you pass the chicken? And we also need the quince paste up here."

A few plates changed places, and Far arranged them around him. It was the best meal Tjor had ever had in his life. For someone who claimed to be unfamiliar with the cuisine of Seagard a few weeks ago, Far knew precisely what went well with what. He drew Tjor into conversations with the other members to make him feel part of the company. They appeared friendly enough, but while the others wanted him to feel less nervous, the grey-haired man called Rav and the Waterhorse held back, watching his every move, like concerned parents sending signals to a prospective son-in-law.

At last, Far pushed his plate away and asked, "Do you want to see the theatre? It should be empty now. I can show you around."

Tjor noticed the worry in Rav's face and shrugged. "If I'm allowed in there?"

"I'll tell everyone you're new. They all know we're looking for another Sorcerer to join us. Saran can't be expected to fill in all the time, not for the traditional roles anyway. Come, let me show you."

Tjor rose to his feet and pulled his cloak from the back of the chair. "If you're sure that it's a good idea."

"I've never had a good idea in my life." Far stuck out his tongue at the others and pulled Tjor into the corridor.

"You don't even have a jacket," Tjor protested. "At least take my cloak. It's bound to be cold outside." He held out the heavy cloth.

Far took his wrist, quickly glancing over his shoulder. "I'm going to kiss you now, if that's fine with you."

Tjor took a step towards him, and they met in the middle.

Tjor had always imagined his first kiss in a chapel in front of a priest, a chaste kiss for a girl his parents had picked out for him and his sister had signed off on, something that was part of the whole respectable package. The corridor in the *Broken Ladle* was dark and smelly and Far's body pressed against him, his arms pulling Tjor so close he could barely breathe. He gave a surprised little jolt as their tongues touched for the first time. If someone had given him the choice, he would have kept kissing Far for the rest of his life. It felt so much better than anything he'd ever thought possible, but of course they had to be careful: the *Ladle* was still in Seagard, still not safe, and so he was only a tiny bit disappointed when Far released him from their embrace. Far folded Tjor's fingers into his and stroked his thumb across the back of Tjor's hand. "I wish you would let me know you better."

Tjor knew exactly what he meant. "Where could we go?" His voice was hoarse, gravelly.

"I'll come up with something," Far promised. "Are you still up for seeing the theatre?"

Tjor knew he would follow Far anywhere, just on the off chance they could kiss again. "Yes, of course. Show me."

They ran down the rickety stairs into the yard of the inn, through a gate reserved for the guests of the *Ladle*. It opened into the garden behind the playhouse. A single lantern was fixed to the back of the building, and they followed the light through a tiny orchard of twisted trees.

It had started to rain. Icy puddles began to form on the cobblestones. They passed two men with brooms and buckets who had just finished giving the stage a once-over. Far exchanged a few pleasant words, but neither of them queried the player's presence. Another lantern hung on a nail above the entrance to the pit. At night the Crooked Lane playhouse was dark and enormous, full of never-ending shadows, like a yawning maw leading to the Underworld.

Tjor stepped in front of the stage and shuddered. The empty galleries looming over them were menacing, jutting out above, the perfect hiding place for mischievous spirits. The whole place had soaked up words for years, all those stories of Witches and Evil Kings and Waterhorses; it had waited for him to enter at the hand of the Fairy, to be tempted.

6
SOMETHING WORTH RISKING

"HOW MANY TIMES DID you kiss him?" Tjovis asked.

"Just the once—for a long time though."

It had become a lot colder overnight. The Longest Night of the year was not so far away, and tiny snowflakes had begun to fall in the evening, coating the cobbles on the Blue Bridge with a thin grey layer, easily worn away by the students coming to the Company houses from all over town.

He had met his sister at the side of Seagard harbour as promised. She wore the furry hat, the hood of a thick ankle-length woollen cloak pulled over it. She looked like the mysterious lady in an adventure novel and must've drawn a lot of attention wandering about the streets like that, on her own.

The closest reputable chocolate house was *The Fat Mouse*, near Mousegate. The only Company that accepted girls were the Unicorns; the *Mouse* was associated with them and full of young women in blue student robes. They knew he did not belong with them, but it was a place where his sister fit in. She paid upfront so he could stop worrying about the time.

They sat down at a small table at the back of the room. The chocolate was not quite as sweet as in the *Macaroon* but not what he wanted after a strenuously boring morning in the office, one in which he had had such trouble concentrating on every loop his goose feather quill scratched onto the eggshell-coloured paper used for the records. He had waited for the releasing sound of the break bell, stumbled out of the House of the Gulls, and was so relieved to find that Tjovis was on time. She had led him to the *Mouse,* and he'd talked about what had happened, knowing he would not be able to explain the details as soon as they were seated inside. She was about to leave Aunt Alis's to go home for the celebrations; he would be left alone to wait for the next time he could escape into Westown.

"When will you meet again?" She cut one of the lemon squares into even smaller pieces.

"I don't know. He said he'll put my name on the list at the playhouse so I can come and see the play again, but I already had a weird comment today from one of the senior clerks because I didn't eat dinner at the refectory. I didn't know they had my name on their list to check on."

She rubbed the bridge of her nose. "Tjor ...."

"I know. I'll be careful."

"No, I mean you can't let them stop you. You only have a few days left before they leave Crooked Lane."

He attempted a tired smile. "Any new candidates in sight for you?"

She made a dismissive gesture with the bowl still in her hand and spilled some chocolate on the tablecloth. "Not new ones. He asked again though. I think Aunt Alis might've encouraged him; she obviously doesn't see any problem with keeping it in the family."

"Lots of the Founding Families marry their cousins."

Her eyes narrowed. "I'm not going to. End of discussion."

"You don't have anyone else in mind?"

"No." She put down the bowl and bent closer to him. "Have you ever wondered about the girls who learn in the House of the Unicorns? They must be of the Founding Families. Will they go on to travel the world like their brothers or will they finish their education and go back into their manor houses and wish they were still on the Bridge?"

Tjor listened to the voices around them, the laughter and clinking of porcelain against teeth, the rustle of robes and opening and closing of books. Happy noises, as far as he could tell. "Would you have liked to be one of them?"

Tjovis shrugged. "It was never an option. I haven't really thought about it, but it seems strange that I can sit in the same room as them as long as I have the silver to buy cakes. They don't look that different from us."

"Not that different from you," he corrected. "They all know I'm not supposed to be here. Some days I wish ...." He brushed a few crumbs off the table.

"Well, of course I could catch the eye of someone fabulously rich—one of the eccentric lords, say. I still have two days left before I go back and everyone returns home for the feast days. There must be a wealth of eligible men coming to Seagard to see their mommies. That could be fun."

"I suppose Father would be happy."

She grimaced. "No, he wouldn't. He needs me to find someone who can help in the business. Are all of the senior clerks married?"

"Don't even joke about it," he growled.

She walked him back to the Bridge. Coming down the sloping main street, the first things they saw were the masts of the sailing ships; not all berths were occupied but now that it had started to snow, the ships would stay longer, some of them moving to the dry docks to be repaired over winter.

To the right, the Blue Bridge with the four Company Houses was busy. Many people had taken their break away from the offices and were returning. For anyone visiting the city, it seemed like a scene anyone would want to be part of, bustling and colourful. *I wish I could truly belong here*, Tjor thought.

Tjovis gave him a hug. "Don't let them push you down. We'll see each other soon. You haven't cancelled your plans?"

He shook his head.

She sighed. "Good. I'll need you there. Mother won't shut up about ... everything."

He kissed and released her. "A few of us are going east. I already paid for the carriage. I'm not looking forward to it though."

"We'll get through it together," she promised.

The rest of the day was hard to endure. Tjor was closing his inkhorn and drying the quills when one of his colleagues put a piece of paper on his desk. It was untidily folded and sealed with candlewax. The message had been scrawled in graphite pen: *Wait at Crooked Gate*.

He stuffed it into his shoulder bag, wrapped his cloak around himself, and ran out of the office. He had so often promised to be careful, but he knew he was being noticed. Sending a letter to the House of the Gulls was not a discreet thing to do. He might not be interesting enough for the students and apprentices, but the other clerks certainly kept tabs on him. He wouldn't get away with it for long. Far and Tjor would have to find a more clandestine method, something like a fixed time, a fixed place.

The snow had decided to stick around, piling up on the tiled roofs of the Harbour Quarter and next to the walls of the merchant houses lining the main street. He was becoming familiar with even more shortcuts, able to reach Crooked Gate before the next bells. He shook snow from the woolly hat that was part of his winter uniform and leant onto a ledge in the wall. Many of the thoroughfares were built in, once used by carriages driving into the mews of bigger houses, before the gardens were dug over to be used for new tenements.

He had just crossed his arms when the woman he'd seen with the players stepped into the gate. She saw his surprise and smiled. "Just a precaution."

He knew what she meant. Anyone who thought it wise to follow him would see him meeting her instead. He smiled back. "Thank you."

She took his arm as Tjovis had done earlier and steered him away from the playhouse, back towards Eastown. So many people were involved in his love life, people he had not even known existed two days ago yet formed a protective shell around them both. If they loved Far so fiercely, maybe he was worthy of the same response? They clearly did not think worse of Far because he was interested in Tjor. They must have their own rules. It made him feel better, if not quite safe.

She did not walk quickly, and they performed a few squiggles through some of the smaller lanes before they came upon a storage yard. It took him a few moments to understand they had circled back on themselves and arrived somewhere behind the Crooked Lane playhouse. He could see the medlar trees in the orchard, with some of the round fruit still clinging to their bare branches.

She led him up a set of stairs at the back of the yard. Far was waiting for him, sitting on a laundry basket. "Sorry for the subterfuge. Thank you, Malis."

The woman closed the door behind him and left them alone together.

Far stood up to face him. "Jom mentioned you were probably leaving town for the holidays, and I panicked." He put his hands around Tjor's face. Far was wearing mittens and a flat hat with earflaps, but he still felt cold to the touch. He must've been waiting for quite some time. They kissed very carefully, both not quite trusting the other not to turn around and storm out.

Tjor pulled the mittens off and warmed Far's hands between his own. "Have you got a lot of performances coming up for the festivities?" he asked.

"They scheduled a few extra ones. We won't have time to sleep in between." Far looked over his shoulder into the back of the room. "It's not ideal, but there are a few blankets and a bit of space between the crates. Maybe one day there will be a proper bed for us, with pillows. For now, this is the best I could do. I'm sorry."

"It's fine. I doubt I'll concentrate much on the décor."

Far grinned and unpinned the iron brooch from Tjor's cloak. He moved slowly around Tjor and pulled the fabric off his shoulders, then put his arms around Tjor and held him against his chest, standing on his toes to be able to kiss Tjor's neck.

It felt important to warn Far. "My knees are going wobbly."

"That means I'm doing it right. You're very warm and my fingers still cold ...." Far started on the buttons of the uniform while nuzzling into him.

Tjor closed his eyes, allowing himself to trust that all would be well, that he would not embarrass himself too much, that Far would not be disgusted by him, that Tjovis had been right, and that love was something worth risking his life and everything else for.

7
BETWEEN CHORES

Two days later, Tjor sat on top of a very rickety carriage on the East Road out of Seagard. Six apprentices of the Gulls had squeezed themselves inside with a basket of delicacies that gave off such a strong smell of pickled onions, he was almost relieved to not have to share the interior of the carriage with them, though it kept snowing and the icy wind tried to unseat him whenever the vehicle came to a gap in the line of trees that protected the road from the worst of the sea breezes.

In the summer, his journey would've been quicker; he might have kept the money and walked instead. The powerful grey team trotted along, unfazed by the weather, the coachman obviously used to the route.

There were a lot of smaller towns and villages on the east coast that guaranteed enough passengers at every time of year, and the coachman must have felt lucky to be engaged by the Honourable Company of the Gulls, sure to receive a better price from them.

The other clerk next to Tjor on the top bench looked barely human, more like a snow-dusted caterpillar: he wore three coats, a massive shawl, and a slouchy hat pulled way past his eyebrows. He probably had a very long way to go. Tjor was glad he only had a few more miles to endure and kept himself occupied with memories of his time in the storeyard.

He had not seen Far since. They both had been too busy preparing for the most important days of the year, when almost everybody tried to get home to be with their families when the new year arrived—the only week when the office closed properly. Of course, his colleagues found a multitude of tasks for him to finish before it did. Meanwhile Far was rehearsing two new plays and finishing off the successful run of the old one.

There was nothing else to do but remember how Far's hands had felt, and how his mouth had moved on Tjor, and that for a moment he really thought he'd blacked out, the release had been so intense. He knew that whatever happened in the new year, just thinking about the boy in his arms would let him know there was a person he could be, someone who had been held and kissed, who was never even asked to change for the privilege—not to be less clumsy, less weird, or better dressed. Afterwards they had talked for a while. Far had spoken of the village he'd left behind deep in a half-forgotten valley up north, and how he still felt guilty of running away, even after all these months. It was likely that the company would return to the Hillakes the next year, and Far was afraid to go home. He had left before the shearing. That was not something he expected to be forgiven for.

Tjor had held him close, but it was so cold in the storeroom that their breath was visible around them, and in the end, they had to get up and dressed. They had said their goodbyes in front of *The Broken Ladle*, and then Far had turned away to join the others in preparation for their evening performance.

The carriage approached the fork in the road. Tjor would have to be a grateful son as soon as he stepped into his father's house. The truth was, as disappointed as he'd been with how his life in Seagard had turned out before Far, he'd never wanted to come back to Applebeck, that handful of houses clustered around the cider mill with its trading office next to the butcher's yard and the bakery, while everyone pretended they lived just next to the big city. In Seagard none of them could've afforded to rent a house half the size they were used to out here. The people in the centre of the village looked down on the farmers that lived further east, and the farmers despised the villagers, so everyone kept themselves occupied. His father, as one of the men involved in running the mill, always seemed to be in the middle of it. He had wanted Tjor to escape, albeit in a way that made his family look good.

The driver let him jump off in front of the mill, among the men who were loading up the last barrels due to be delivered for the holidays. Snow covered the roofs of the houses, making everything look much cleaner than usual, but the smell of fermented apples hung over the road. When the carriage passed him on its way to the other side of the village, he stared after it and the wrapped-up people sitting on top. He had the impulse to run after it and jump on again, but he had only paid to be brought home, and now he was home.

His father's house was situated close to the village chapel, a prime location, and had an extensive vegetable garden, its own apple orchard, and a low-sloping roof, thatched, with windows peeking out from the tightly packed straw. The girl who helped in the house came around the corner with a basket of logs for the fires and gave a little cry. The door ripped open and his sister hurtled across the snow.

"Thank Heavens! I need you to step in and tell her there is no way I'm going to marry him. Ever since I've come back, I haven't heard the end of it." She pushed him towards the house, huffing and puffing. The dark, narrow hall was made even smaller by the mass of coats and shawls hung up at the entrance. He shook the snow from his clothes. It took some time until he freed himself, left his own cloak to dry, and followed Tjovis into the kitchen, where their mother was helping the cook stretch the dough for the cake that was part of the traditional celebration in Applebeck, one stuffed with currants and highly spiced with cinnamon, allspice, cloves, and ginger—something Far surely would've loved.

"You are late." His mother finished hooking the paper-thin dough around the corners of the kitchen table, wiped her hands down her apron, and then thought better of hugging him. "Did you have anything to do with that?" She gestured towards his sister.

He slowly shook his head. "I've not spoken to Aunt Alis since the first week I came to town, and she still hasn't invited me back to the house."

His mother narrowed her eyes at him. "You should get out of that uniform. I've laid out some clothes for you. I hope you've not put on weight again. We can't afford to—"

"I've brought some of my own clothes," he interrupted her.

"Why? The chests are full of your old stuff. Go and wash your face."

"He's going to have some tea first," decided his sister. "I'll get it, just sit down in the backroom."

He nodded, but his skin crawled. He longed to turn around and jump into the snowdrift next to the turnip bed. He had not been in the house for a minute, and he already wanted to cry.

The backroom smelled of wet leather and the pinecones heaped into the hearth. As usual, it was the coldest room in the house; it was where they came when they could not allow themselves to get comfortable, when they only had time for a little break between chores. He sank down on one of the wooden stools and rubbed his hands.

Tjovis appeared with a tray. "It still needs to brew a bit." She sat next to him. "Mother's been in a mood all day. All the preparations …. We've been on our feet since dawn." She filled the earthenware bowls for them. "Mother has a whole list for you, so be prepared." Tjovis touched his stubbly cheek. "You look tired."

"I spent hours on the winter roads, freezing on the roof of a carriage." He tried sipping the tea, but it was still too hot; he almost burned his mouth. "I suppose Father is still in the mill? It looked as if a lot of consignments were going out."

"He's using the opportunity to keep away from the house as much as possible. There's been a lot of swearing in the evenings, though. You might start to miss your office very soon."

"How are you, Tjovis?"

"Apart from the whole proposal debacle?" She leant her forehead on his shoulder. "Thank you for being here. I can't suppress five screaming fits a day. Wasn't this holiday meant to be peaceful and quiet?"

"Perhaps for the priests. I wish we could lock one of them in the kitchen with her for the last weeks before the Longest Night."

"Oh, they've learnt to avoid us. The new one tried to visit a few times when he was sent over from Market Temple, but he gave up rather quickly. Regrettably, he was the pretty one. I like them dormouse-y."

Tjor chuckled quietly into his collar. "Would you have married him?"

She shrugged. "Why not? He seemed nice. But then I'd probably end up living just across the road."

He tried the tea again, and it was finally cool enough to drink. He tasted the mixture of herbs his mother preferred, strong and very sweet. He would never have the chance to live happily married across the road from his parents. Bringing Far to Applebeck was out of the question. Tjor's mother called for him from the kitchen. He flinched and finished his tea in a few gulps.

The first afternoon Tjor mostly spent up a ladder in the sitting room, putting up the bunting and garlands of holly, ivy, and mistletoe. The next morning, he was sent to the butcher's with the handcart from the gardens to collect their order, plus a cask of apple brandy from the mill's trading office. At least the errand got him out of the house, and after returning the cart, he climbed over the garden fence and crossed the graveyard to the chapel.

His boots left deep impressions in the snow. He was sweating when he reached the building with the copper star fixed on the gable. In the months he'd been in Seagard, he hadn't set foot into one of the big city temples, but this was the chapel he was used to, from being pushed into it every third day for the shorter services. Like all families in the village, the na Tialins had to demonstrate their devotion.

It felt good to be alone for an hour before he allowed himself to be drawn into his family's world again. As always, the door stuck a bit in winter, and he had to lean against it to enter the whitewashed room filled with polished wooden seats, its walls painted with red and yellow ochre in patterns of flowers, stars, and the moon in all its phases.

The chapel of Applebeck was already decorated in the same style as the house, prepared for the ritual that would bring in the new year. The door fell into the frame behind him with a creak that made him break out in goosebumps. It might help him to get through Longest Night now that he'd seen the place again before the ceremony, before he had to sit still and hold onto his thoughts, as he had done so many lonely years before.

8
GET THROUGH THE NIGHT

O F ALL THE RITUALS Tjor had been subjected to during his life, he hated the Wake on the Longest Night the most. He did not need a whole night set aside to think about everything wrong with him and his life, and suffering through all those hours among family had always been painful.

When he turned his back on the chapel and made his way down the path to the official exit from the yard, the wind had picked up. He shivered on the snow-covered road, passing a few villagers who gave him meaningful nods. Maybe they could imagine what it felt like to come home from the city for the holidays.

He tried to re-enter the family house as quietly as possible, but his mother stuck her head out of the kitchen. "You're late. Your father wants to see you."

For a moment he had trouble breathing. He didn't need to ask where to go. His father had long reserved part of the house for his particular use, a room as large as the common sitting room and sparsely furnished. There were a desk, two chairs, and one seat by the fireplace, where his father now dried his boots.

Tjor slowly closed the door behind him. "Father?"

Tjovis and Tjor took after their mother's family; his father was a lot smaller than him, with a close-cropped sandy beard. He pointed at one of the chairs. "Sit."

He always made Tjor sit down.

"They've been sending the reports through." His father had a slow, deep voice. His clothes, even after a long day at the mill, looked clean and pressed. Tjor felt ashamed of his own state, his wind-tangled hair. He hastily tried to smooth it down.

"They're saying you've been working hard." His father stood up and took a little leather-covered bottle from his desk. The smell of apple brandy leapt into the room. "It won't be too long before they give you a raise." He pushed a tiny pewter cup filled with the golden liquid towards Tjor. "I've shared the news with a few people and we've had offers."

Tjor blinked, the cup halfway to his mouth. "Offers?"

"Your mother is very keen to see you married. She has opinions on the girls, of course. My advice is to let her make the first selection."

Tjor's mouth felt terribly dry. "You don't think it's too early?"

"Your sister is a year younger than you and she's been prepared for a long time. Soon you'll be able to afford renting your own rooms in the city, and everyone wants to leave for Seagard. You have some days to think it over. I believe your mother wants you to run a few more errands."

Tjor rose to his feet, put the cup he hadn't drunk from on the windowsill behind him, and left his father's room without another word.

Tjor had the chance to tell Tjovis at the end of the day, when they were sent upstairs to get ready for the ritual. She was less sympathetic than expected. "At least that prospect will keep you awake today."

He gasped. "That's not funny!"

"How do you think I've felt for the last two years? I might not be the only one who ends up marrying a cousin." She shook her head. "Sorry. I know it's a lot to wrap your head around."

"It feels as if the walls are closing in." *Or as if I'm slowly being strangled.*

"I really don't know why they started pushing you so early."

"They know something happened."

"How would they know?"

"Because I've felt guilty since I jumped off the carriage." *Because they smell the hope on me.*

"You always feel guilty; that can't be it. Calm down. She can't read your mind."

"I'm sure she's trying to." *I'm sure she can.*
"Get changed now. I'll help you later."

Tjor wished his father had waited, but he might have done it on purpose, to provide him with a clearer future to contemplate during the Wake. Who on Earth had volunteered their daughters to marry him? Had the daughters themselves had any say in it? Judging by the discussions between Tjovis and their mother, no one valued their opinion. That kind of fear was new to him, but his sister had lived with it for years. No wonder she reacted as she did.

He managed to put his best clothes on: black woollen trousers, a clean grey linen shirt, and a jacket with a lot of buttons that he could just about do up. He waited for Tjovis to knock and let herself in, but it took her a long time. He was about to go and search for her when she came quietly into the room, a sturdy wooden comb in her right hand. She looked as if she'd been crying and gave him a hug. The house around them had gone eerily quiet; everyone was preparing, and the serving girl and the cook had left to make their way to their own families.

Tjovis had a hard time getting through the knots in his hair. "Do you want me to tidy the ends?"

He shook his head. "I'm going to tie it back anyway." He smiled at her. "You look nice."

"It'd better look nice. It's a new dress; took me ages to finish." She patted down her dark blue apron. "Will you get through the night?"

His smile withered. "Will you?"

"Not if I have to worry about my big brother."

"I'm serious, Tjovis. I'm sorry I can't be here all the time and keep her off you."

She snorted, very unladylike. "I don't need you for that. I can take her."

Of course she was lying. They always lied to make each other feel better.

He followed her down the stairs. Candles had been lit in the hall. The whole house smelled of honey and pine needles. He opened the front door. The procession had started from the village, every single person bringing a light with them to the chapel of Applebeck. It was a beautiful sight; he could almost forget the ordeal all of them had to get through to start the new year under the eyes of the Gods. It was a clear, frosty evening, and the sky hung full of stars. They would be cold hours to sit through.

From the back of the hall his mother let out a shriek. "We're late!"

The family had their own bench in the respectable bit of the room, and like every year, his mother shot disapproving looks at everyone who had brought a cushion. They filed in and sat down; there wasn't much space for Tjor's knees, and like every year, he had to sit turned slightly sideways. By the end of the night, he would be in agony.

As soon as people arrived, they stopped talking, as was the custom. In a few moments every candle would be snuffed out, and they would hold the Wake in absolute silence until sunrise. It was important that the family was seen attending the ritual.

He was tempted to look around, to find out if there were any young women staring at him with quiet despair, but he kept his eyes fixed on the back of the bench in front of him. He could not afford to be the cause of malicious gossip in Applebeck. When the lights were extinguished, the darkness washed over him in a wave of relief.

He awoke when his sister dug her elbow into his ribs. He had been leaning on the wall of the chapel. He couldn't have lasted long, and his father must've noticed him falling asleep. He might interpret it as Tjor taking a well-earned rest from his exhausting life in the city, or—and this was most likely—as his son embarrassing him in front of everyone.

Tjor rubbed his face, stifling a yawn. At least he felt calmer now. He must've missed a good few hours of the Wake. A grey glimmer of light came through the windows. He only had two more days before he could return to the city with a whole day off to spend as he wished. He had arranged to meet Far at the playhouse.

Had Far managed to stay awake? It would've been his only free night of the holidays. The players probably held their private Wake in *The Broken Ladle,* or perhaps they'd decided to join a congregation in one of the smaller chapels in the Westown. Would their prayers differ from those of the people of Applebeck? Or did they all hope for the same thing in the end?

Would Far have found the time to think about him at all? In the middle of multiple performances, the rehearsals? Would Far want to think about him?

Tjor shoved his hands underneath his thighs and tried to relieve his numb behind. He had to trust in Far. He could not allow himself to sit in the icy light of the new year's first sunrise and doubt the one good thing that had happened to him in the city. Far had been the one asking about their next meeting after they'd kissed goodbye in the storehouse. Surely nothing could've come to pass in the last few days that would cause Far to re-evaluate their relationship?

He desperately screwed his eyes shut. His sister's sharp elbow caught him again. A low hum had started from the benches behind them, the sign that the Wake was about to end, that they had lived through the cold lonely hours once more, to arise in the new light.

The two village priests stood up from their seats and began to sing the first hymn of the year. They had been trained at Market Temple; their voices were beautiful and filled the chapel, but when the rest of the congregation was allowed to join in, Tjor remained silent.

Laughter and applause swept through the room. Now they were all permitted to break their fast with the celebration dishes they had spent days, if not weeks, preparing. People rose to their feet, massaging their cramping thighs and hugging each other. His mother stepped into the next bench to speak with the neighbours, his father standing awkwardly by her side.

Tjovis turned to him and held out her hand. "Happy new year."

Neither of them looked particularly happy, but he nodded. "Happy new year. Let's go outside and look at the sky."

They could see a few clouds, the sun rising fast over the hills. Tjovis stood next to him, her hair dishevelled, as if she'd spent some time with her head in her hands.

He carefully cleared his throat. "Have you decided?"

"Yes. You?"

"Yes. I think I have."

9
ANOTHER OPTION

IT WAS STRANGE TO come back to town with the holidays still going on. The streets were unusually quiet; the carriage Tjor arrived in was one of the very few vehicles around. He had been allowed to travel inside because of a spare seat and had not even needed to pay the difference.

He arrived late at White Bear Yard. Someone had cleaned his room while he was away. The sheets on the bed were fresh and the dust under the washstand gone. He ate the food he'd brought from home—pieces of the infamous currant cake, eel pie, saffron biscuits, and cinnamon buns—then unlaced his boots and crawled into the clean bed.

When he awoke with the sun the next day, he was astonished to find that he'd slept long and deep for the first time in weeks. He washed, dressed, and left the Yard, picking up a bag of sticky almond cakes on his way into Westown. The good weather had prevailed, a most unusual event during the Longest Night holiday. He saw a lot of people on their way to meet up with families and friends, wearing their finest clothes for the occasion. Everyone wanted to make the best out of the last day before the whole city went back to work. But Far and the company had worked all the way through, and when Tjor reached Crooked Lane, the streets were filled with people waiting for the first performance of the day.

He made his way to the man selling the tickets and gave his name.

"Ah, yes. They said you're supposed to go 'round the back'." He whistled to a boy at the hazelnut stall and gave him instructions.

Tjor followed the boy into the playhouse.

The last time he had seen the empty building was at night. Now the whole house seemed ready and waiting. The pit was swept clean; colourful banners were displayed from the top gallery and rustled expectantly. The boy renting out the seat cushions was already at his post arranging the stacks, and gave him a little wave.

The last time he had been there, the rooms at the back of the stage had been dark and empty; now they were crammed with people. The company was squashed together in their costumes, fiddling with paint and hair needles.

Malis helped with Far's curls, carefully arranging them, then scooping up a handful of the blue silk flowers that belonged to the Fairy from the Hill.

Far's face was painted a stark, unearthly white, with dark powder along the ridge of his nose and under the cheekbones. He turned to Tjor and smiled. Malis grabbed the back of his head and turned him around again. "We're at the critical stage. Don't move again or I'll ram one of them into your head. Nice to see you again, Tjor. How was your time at home?"

Tjor sank onto one of the costume chests lined up next to them. "Horrible, but I knew it would be."

Far tried to look at him without turning his head, like a horse searching for a reason to spook. "What happened?"

Tjor folded his hands together. "Nothing much. The usual family stuff."

Malis gave him a quick disapproving look, and Tjor blushed. None of the players had been able to spend time with their own families, and Far must have missed his. "Sorry," he mumbled. "I fell asleep during the Wake and got a stern talking-to from both my parents afterwards."

"I fall asleep every time." Saran joined in, wearing the sober black clothes the Waterhorse meets the Prince in for the first time. His face had already been made up, his mouth powdered over with rice flour so that he looked ghastly and stern. He walked over to Far and laid a hand on his shoulder. Tjor saw the fingers squeeze briefly, then release. It must've been some sort of signal. The last of the flowers were poked in and secured with wire, then Far looked up at the Waterhorse and nodded. Both Saran and Malis stepped back and everyone else seemed to give them space.

Far shuffled his chair around to face him. Now that he was ready to go on stage, there was no question of them kissing. Tjor's heart leapt into his throat. "You look beautiful."

"Fairies are supposed to be beautiful. Thank you for coming back."

"Why wouldn't I come back?"

"I was afraid I might've scared you off after the last time." Far gestured towards his fellow players. "They've been taking bets."

"Bets that I wouldn't come back?" Tjor felt stunned. "But I love you."

Far's dark eyes widened. All movement in the room ceased.

Tjor counted three heartbeats before everyone started talking loudly, hiding Far's reply in a sea of voices. "I love you too. I think. It all happened very quickly, but I know it'll break my heart to leave you behind." Far's hands were covered in greasepaint, but he reached out and touched Tjor's face anyway. "I might not be able to. Everyone is getting worried about it. Rav and Saran think there might be another option."

"Another option?"

"Have you ever thought about becoming one of us?"

"One of you? You mean being ... on stage?" The blood drained from Tjor's face.

"We still haven't found our Evil Sorcerer and Saran said, maybe you want to audition?"

"But everyone would be looking at me."

"Tjor, everyone already looks at you."

"And I hate it!" *It makes me want to die.*

"Just think about it. We would have time to train you. Saran agreed to let me play the Queen in the next one, but at some point, he obviously wants to switch again."

Tjor stared at him. "I don't believe I can, Far."

"Don't decide yet, please. Watch the play today and let me know later. It's only an idea, only a ...."

His voice cracked. For a moment they sat in silence.

Tjor swallowed. "When do you have to know?"

"Our engagement runs out in four days. We're going north from here, a manor house near Troutbourne and then on to Greengard to stay for the rest of the winter."

"Greengard!" He knew the name from many of the records he copied. The Gulls had one of the most successful stations up in Greengard, but he would never have the opportunity to transfer there, and of course, winter would end, and the company would move again. He would lose them.

The noises in the room had changed. The audience must've begun to stream into the playhouse. Far rose to his feet. "There's a seat you can use," he said, "if you don't mind watching the whole thing again. It's not technically meant for audience members but for people helping with the sets and the light and noise effects. Come, I'll show you."

Tjor followed the Fairy from the Hill across the room, dazed and deeply unhappy at the same time. A narrow door led from the area behind the stage to the first-floor gallery, into a space with an empty bench and enough room to store a few props, but for this play it had been kept empty. It was not a great spot; he had to bend his neck to see the full stage. He turned around to thank Far, but he had already left. Some people were looking at him; maybe they thought him part of the play. He quickly sat down.

The pit was filling up more and more. He could not see any students or apprentices. During the holidays, the tickets were double the price. Most of the audience were probably on their way back from their families. Maybe some of them had come in the clothes they wore at home; even the people in the pit looked cleaner today. The bench he sat on was uncomfortably low, but he was almost too distracted to notice.

How had he been able to declare his love *and* deny them their future at the same time? Backing off so quickly, before he'd given it a chance? Merely the possibility of crossing the line had made him panic. It was the world of the players, people who wanted to speak in front of lots of others, who *longed* to be the centre of attention. Far wanted to be where he was, he had left his family for the opportunity to step into this life, and all Tjor desired was to stay hidden. Especially after the excruciating days in Applebeck, after leaving his sister behind again.

He barely noted the music starting. The gates of the playhouse had closed, and a hush fallen over the audience. The Young King and the Prince came on stage. Now he knew the names of both of those men, had eaten with them. When the scene changed to the Hill and Far walked into the middle of the stage, the house erupted into applause. Perhaps he was not the only one watching the play for the second time. All those people seemed to know who Far was, how good he was. Far had become famous in Seagard, and though he had sounded so sad and disappointed mere moments ago, now he shone with the same confidence that had made Tjor fall in love with him. He surely was not the only one who admired the Fairy; some in the audience must be willing to give everything to deserve his attention. They had not kissed him yet; they had not slept with him between the crates. Far had not followed any of them into an expensive chocolate house just to speak with them, to find out their name. They would've given anything to be in Tjor's position, to be the one whom Far wanted enough to ask him to stay.

Tjor had been kept afraid all his life, by his father, his mother, the priests in the chapel, the senior clerks at the office.

The audience laughed at the Fairy and her Servant, and applauded again when their scene ended. Tjor rushed to his feet, pushed against the door. It stuck and he had to ram against it, when it suddenly opened and he stumbled into the room at the back of the stage.

Far stood in the wings, fiddling with his hair, his eyes cast down to the floor. When Tjor banged his knee against one of the chests littering the room, Far looked up and their eyes met.

He mouthed, "You're supposed to stay back there."

Tjor shook his head. "I won't."

EPILOGUE
GETTING AWAY

IT'S ONE OF THE most famous stories. I can't believe you don't know it."

"There are lots of things people growing up in Applebeck don't know." Tjor tried to move around on the hard seat. At least it was high enough for him.

Far squinted against the bright light. He still wore traces of kohl around his eyes. "It takes place in a castle overlooking Lightwater, way back when the continent was split into lots of independent kingdoms. The king is very busy travelling from one end of the land to the other and leaves his young wife behind."

He smirked. "She puts up with it for a couple of years but then gets horribly bored and goes for a ride. She meets a young shepherd and of course they fall in love, as people do. She starts plotting against her husband, even seduces one of his noble followers so he thinks she'll marry him. The evil duke kills the king, but the queen wants the shepherd to sit next to her on the throne, and all the noblemen revolt against her, led by the duke. She's desperate enough to call on the water sprites in the lake for help, but of course the sprites try to get around the deal, and she ends up having to fight both them and the noble families."

Tjor stared at Far's gloved hands, dancing around as he told the story. "Even the shepherd tries to reason with her. In the end, she loses the kingdom and is sentenced to be drowned. But then the sprites call in their debt and pull her into the lake—she has to marry their prince. That is where she lives to this day, and it's why sometimes weird lights can be seen in the water. It's the queen, dancing with her new husband under the waves, wishing she was back on land."

Far sighed happily. "It was always my favourite, maybe because we lived so close to the Lightwater lake and the shepherd could well have been related to me. Most stage versions show her as bitter and jealous, wicked and lustful, but Rav puts a different spin on it." He gestured towards the player. "I tried to explain how I've always seen her, as someone very disappointed with her life and willing to risk everything to feel loved again." He rubbed his mittens together. "Rav thinks I can play her in a way that makes you wish she would succeed. He wants to start you off as one of the sprites, to see how that goes."

They had passed the Northgate some time ago. Now that the holidays were over and the quiet days of the new year had begun, when everybody tried to keep their heads down and get back into their work, they met few people.

It had not snowed for the last four days; the sky was a glassy blue with thin clouds and a watery sun, but the wind coming over the fields made riding up front on the wagon uncomfortable, though Far had pulled down some of the tarpaulin to create a more sheltered space for Jom at the reins. They made slow progress, the spiked horseshoes crunching into the compacted snow and the visible breath of the horses floating up towards them.

Tjor had had his official audition for the company only two days ago. Far had been there to read with him, and Tjor had stood on the same dusty stage, looking up to where he and Tjovis had sat on their first night, eating hazelnuts and catching up on the latest family drama, without realizing everything was about to change.

Far had tried to make it easy for him, picking a scene from one of the stories they both knew. Tjor had not been in costume, but Far had given him a wide-brimmed hat with a fluffy plume, the sort of hat that came with a personality of its own. As soon as it touched Tjor's head, he felt his posture change. His chest expanded, his shoulders relaxed, and for the first time in many years he stood as tall as he had grown, as if something that had cowered in his soul finally received a leg up. *I* can *be other people*, Tjor had realized in astonishment. *I've been other people for a long time to survive.*

Afterwards they'd left Rav, Saran, and the Wise King to talk. He knew that he merely needed to be good enough to be considered and had felt the shift as soon as he spoke the words Far had made him learn. He was already tall, black-haired, green-eyed, and the hat brought out the rest of the Pirate Prince. It had not been a great surprise when he'd received their written offer.

He had handed in his notice at the Gulls the next morning, his uniform folded and wrapped in the pillowcase from his bed in the Yard. He'd written his letters; his last salary would be sent to his parents in full, but he folded his remaining silver coin into the letter he addressed to his sister. He brought it to Aunt Alis's after collecting his reference from the office on his last morning in Seagard. Tjovis was expected to arrive in mere days, now that she'd accepted her cousin's hand during the holidays.

The only thing Tjor brought from White Bear Yard was a change of clothes and the box containing his books and the bits and pieces he'd kept from the life he'd left that day, trying not to look back, not to be distracted and caught again.

His last night in Seagard he'd spent in *The Broken Ladle*, in Far's narrow, very creaky bed. He had slept badly, worried someone might find him, that his sister's fiancé was searching the town for him, trying to prevent the scandal that would arise from the decisions Tjor had made since his first day behind the stage. At some point his parents would come to understand that Tjovis had known of the things that had brought the situation about; he was sure they would try to intimidate her and still felt horrible thinking about what he was putting her through, now that he sat on the second of the company's wagons. He was to share it with Jom, Far, and the man who played the Fool.

Tjor heard panting breath behind them, someone running through the snow to catch up. Far craned his neck, beaming at the man waving his mittens.

"Is there space for one?" Saran called to them.

Jom rolled his eyes. "What did you do?"

"Nothing much," the man who played the Waterhorse said. "Malis is in one of her moods. Can you talk to her, Far? She usually listens to you." He pushed a hank of red hair from his face, ruddy with exertion. His breath rose like a cloud from his face, and for some reason he wore a pair of woollen skirts today.

"I can't guarantee that I can make her see sense." Far gave Tjor a nudge to reach out to Saran.

Tjor bent down and let his wrist be grabbed. Saran hauled himself up to the bench, squeezing next to Tjor with a groan. "That was harder than it needed to be." He pulled the shawl loose from his throat, and a faint sheen of sweat glistened on his skin. "You are very squirrelly," he noted. "We're still close enough to jump ship, you know."

Tjor shook his head. "No. I've made my decision."

Saran arched a brow at Far. "Have you told him yet?"

"Told me about what?"

"Don't be mean," Jom said with a glare in Saran's direction. "He'll find out soon enough."

Tjor swallowed painfully. "I would like to know now."

Saran grinned. "You'll never fit back in," he said. "If you leave with us today, you'll learn there are many other ways to live your life than what the inklings tell you is good and proper. Next season, when we come back to Seagard, you'll see the people you used to know, your sister maybe, and not understand how they can tolerate it. Far has been through it. He knows we'll get back to Halfway Station in the summer where his own past awaits."

"That doesn't sound so bad," Tjor mumbled, flinching as a rider passed them. He instinctively turned his face away from the road.

Far said, "You know, they will find you eventually."

Tjor huddled into his scarf, pulled the lucky hat down over his ears. "Yes, but I'd be grateful if it wasn't today."

Saran sniffed. "You'll learn a lot of sword-fighting for the Pirate King. Better pay attention if you're worried about people catching up with you."

"It's nothing like that," Tjor protested.

"It will become something like that," Saran said. "In time. If there's one thing they can't abide, it's someone getting away."

Jom glanced at the three of them. "It won't be too long before we make camp. Far, you should start on your lessons."

Far waved his mittens about. "He wouldn't expect me to write with these on."

"I think you remember what Rav said last time."

Far rolled his eyes. "He should be happy that we have men for all the characters again."

"I'm sure he is." The Prince shoved all four reins into his right hand for a moment, reaching down with his left into a little compartment at the foot of the driver's bench. He pulled out a piece of slate and a pen that was tied to it with a bit of string.

Tjor took it from him, and Saran laughed when he saw the sentence covering it. The letters on the slate were half rubbed out, but Tjor could still decipher what Far had written out twenty times before the slate had been stored away for their engagement in Crooked Lane:

The boy who played the Queen.
The boy who played the Queen.
The boy who played the Queen ....

THE END

ACKNOWLEDGEMENTS

MANY PEOPLE ACCOMPANIED ME along the way and need to be thanked:

Isa, who has lived in the Eastern Cities with me for almost three decades and is probably the only person on this planet who can read my handwriting without breaking a sweat. This one harks back to the old days!

Marlen, who is never afraid to go deep. For knowing me too well to let me have the easy way out and for showing me where the best cake lives and where the fairy waterfalls are.

Dorit, graphic designer and flatmate extraordinaire. For the many late nights in our wonky Hildesheim kitchen, talking about our lives to come. I can't wait for us to go explore again.

Diana, Nicole, and Bouke, who continue to go on the adventure with me. For being friends, fellow writers, and first readers, and for believing that all that bloody effort is worth it.

Elena and the Marshalls, who took me in as part of their bubble and have become my found family in the UK.

Lorna, who teaches me about art and shares my enthusiasm for extraordinary places.

Claudia and the Cabbage Club, who help me make sense of the bewildering country we have all come to live in.

Jenna, fellow writer, who gave me so much encouragement when I needed it most and managed to rein in my panic when things didn't move quickly enough.

Gobion, Hannah, and Ariadne Rowlands, fellow writers and avid readers, who have been of more support than they will ever know. I am so grateful that it's never too late in life to make amazing friends! I'm so excited to work with you on projects that nudge me out of my comfort zone.

Aliya for her invaluable beta-reading insights and for putting up with my weird heroes!

River, for such a wonderful and rewarding copy-editing experience. I'm sorry my brain is in such a muddle between UK and US English!

Nick, for the beautiful cover image that embodies so much for what this novella has come to mean to me.

My parents, for coming around to support the choices I make. For teaching me that life is too short to live in a cage. For being role models for adventurous cooking and travelling, for making me interested in how stuff works and all the books, art, and love—and French cheese!

My brother Henry, who shares the story-telling bug. For all the road trips into the wilderness, storm or no storm, snow or no snow.

And every reader who has joined me on this huge scary adventure that is being an indie author writing what they truly want to write.

C. M. Kuhtz is a nonbinary writer of queer fantasy fiction. They have worked with horses, been a member of Viking reenactment and sword fighting troupes, wrote a PhD thesis on queer identities, and are now employed in academic publishing. They live in Hungerford, Berkshire.

www.cmkuhtz.com
Follow them on Instagram and TikTok:
@carliewritesstuff

MANY HUNDRED YEARS BEFORE FAR MET TJOR ...

Sloe Moon series volume 1

SLOE MOON: TALL TREES
C. M. Kuhtz

203 mm x 127 mm, 324 pages, £12.99
ISBN 978-1-7394032-0-1 paperback
ISBN 978-1-7394032-1-8 ebook

What if the Chosen One doesn't get chosen?

Sloe Moon, youngest child of the ruler of Tall Trees, has always wanted to follow in their father's footsteps and become a famous wizard. Instead they are expected to marry for the good of the Moon family and uphold an age-old alliance. When the opportunity arises for them to travel to the famed wizard council of Goldenlake, Sloe and their best friend Qes set off on a journey that will not only put them in the path of mortal danger but also entangle them with the fate of the Moon's allies, enemies, and the mysterious men from the Eastern Cities, who have come to the land of the families with their own agenda. With so many odds stacked against them, will Sloe be able to fulfil their destiny?

Sloe Moon: Tall Trees is the first volume of a six-part queer fantasy series with a fat, nonbinary protagonist.